M000268626

Written in the Stars

by

Lorie O'Brien

Crissy —
Much love &
many thanks!
♡ Lorie O'Brien

DORRANCE
PUBLISHING CO
EST. 1920
PITTSBURGH, PENNSYLVANIA 15238

The contents of this work, including, but not limited to, the accuracy of events, people, and places depicted; opinions expressed; permission to use previously published materials included; and any advice given or actions advocated are solely the responsibility of the author, who assumes all liability for said work and indemnifies the publisher against any claims stemming from publication of the work.

All Rights Reserved
Copyright © 2019 by Lorie O'Brien

No part of this book may be reproduced or transmitted, downloaded, distributed, reverse engineered, or stored in or introduced into any information storage and retrieval system, in any form or by any means, including photocopying and recording, whether electronic or mechanical, now known or hereinafter invented without permission in writing from the publisher.

Dorrance Publishing Co
585 Alpha Dive
Pittsburgh, PA 15238
Visit our website at www.dorrancebookstore.com

ISBN: 978-1-6453-0539-2
eISBN: 978-1-6453-0705-1

I'd like to thank all of my friends and family who have supported me in this crazy dream of mine to write and publish my first novel. To my sweet friend Claire for being the first to read the rough draft cover to cover. Much love and thanks to my amazing niece Cayla for your input and encouragement. I'm blessed with many amazing friends who have been my cheerleaders throughout this process; Amanda, Keri, Lory, Linda, Desiree, Janet, Brandi, Amanda D, Sarah, and the countless others who have showed support along the way. My two wonderful girls Lauryn and Bethany, who I hope see me as a role model and inspiration, I love you both so much. Finally, my husband Dennis, who without him I wouldn't have been able to do any of this. Thank you babe for having my back, loving me in spite of many nights of endless writing, and for finally reading the book.

None of the events or characters in this novel are real or factual.

Part One

"A guy and a girl can be just friends,
but at one point or another
they will fall for each other...
maybe temporarily, maybe at the wrong time
maybe too late, or maybe forever."

—Dave Matthews

Lindsey

When you're young, you don't expect to meet someone that you'll end up loving for the rest of your life. But I did. I don't think I knew it at the time. I only knew him because he obsessively followed my older sister around begging for her attention, while she blatantly ignored him. I guess sometimes I felt a little sorry for him. He was crazy about her and she wouldn't give him the time of day.

My older sister, according to just about everyone, was absolutely perfect in every way. I lived in the shadow of Rachel, straight-A student, beautifully stunning in her looks naturally, golden child of the family, and the girl that every other girl wanted to be. Except me. I wanted to be seen, not linger in the shadow of my sister.

My junior year of high school, Rachel went off to college, and of course, Dylan followed. Life just kind of went on without them back in Katy, Texas. Katy was on the outskirts of Houston, and a rather large city in and of itself. It was mainly comprised of middle to upper class families with large subdivisions, one after the next all very similar. The houses all seemed to look the same, like monopoly houses all lined up next to each other in rows.

Our school, Katy High School, had an average of three hundred to four hundred students in a graduating class. It was a large campus, more like a college instead of a senior high school.

Just like any other school in the South, especially in the state of Texas, football was like religion in our town. There were football games on Friday nights, pep rallies at school, parties on the weekends, and eventually homecoming weekend.

3

Starting my freshman year and lasting now into my junior year, I'd been seeing someone steady, a junior named Michael. Our relationship was anything but perfect. From the outside we looked like the ideal high school couple. I was the popular cheerleader and he was one of the captains of the football team. Our friends were all part of the popular group…the jocks and the cheerleaders.

Our relationship was a constant flip-flop of breaking up and getting back together. Michael was an incessant flirt and was drop-dead gorgeous. He was tall and lean, not skinny but muscular, with bright blue eyes and dirty blonde hair worn long enough to have just a slight wave to it. Just recently he had grown a goatee and even though I wasn't thrilled about it at first, it was starting to grow on me a little. It gave him a little bit of a "bad boy" look which, I had to be honest, was starting to fit his personality all too well these days.

There wasn't a girl in school that didn't envy me as his girlfriend. And he craved the attention—actually, he thrived on it. As the girl who was always fighting other girls off him with a stick, I was extremely jealous and the majority of our fights stemmed from the attention he received, and gave, to other girls.

On the flip side of that, at five-foot, petite, and voted most popular, most outgoing, and junior class secretary, I was also given a lot of attention from other guys at school. I was oblivious to it. Michael was the only guy I paid any attention to. Ironically, he noticed the attention though, and was usually targeting someone for talking to me, looking at me or even standing near me. Talk about a double standard. It was always okay for him to flirt with other girls, but God forbid anyone even spoke to me.

Homecoming was traditionally a grand event with a whole week of events leading up to the football game under the lights, homecoming dance, and the inevitable after-dance party on Friday night. This year was no exception. That week was full of theme days at school, the traditional homecoming mums worn by the girls from their parents and/or boyfriends, and the Friday pep rally the day of the big game and dance.

As usual I cheered on the sidelines at the game while Michael played alongside his teammates and friends. The stands were filled with students, parents, and faculty there to support the school.

After the game, we went to the dance, and ended up at a party at our friend Chad's house. Chad's parents were always out of town and since he lived only two blocks from my house I could make it home for curfew and then sneak back out after my parents thought I was asleep. Homecoming night was no different. After Michael brought me home, I waited long enough, then climbed out my bedroom window and made the two block walk back to the party. Only when I got there, I had found that Michael had left. I asked my best friend and partner in crime Keri, "Where's Michael?"

Keri and I had been friends since my family moved to the area from New York when I was in third grade. We instantly hit it off as "bff's" in school, being assigned to share a locker on the first day of school. Even more lucky for us, we only lived a few blocks from each other, rode the same bus to and from school, and liked all of the same things. We were practically joined at the hip.

"He left," she said. "Jimmy needed a ride home and he offered to take him."

"Is he coming back?" I asked.

"No, he said to tell you that he wasn't going to drive all the way back and he'll call you tomorrow."

A little irritated I said, "Well, I think we should stay and have a little fun."

I headed into the kitchen to get a drink. I filed through the crowd of mostly friends and a few faces I didn't recognize. Sometimes other schools in the area would catch word of a party and some people would show up that we didn't know.

A group of guys, all friends of Michael's, were playing beer pong, acting ridiculous, and of course keeping an eye on what I was doing and who I was talking to. They would be sure to watch me like a hawk and were most likely told to by Michael. He was overly protective he and his buddies looked out for each other, and that included the girls they were dating.

After an hour or so and a couple of drinks I was tired and ready to head home.

"Keri, I'm going to head out."

"Okay. Do you want me to get Mac and we can take you home?" she asked. "You probably shouldn't walk by yourself."

"I'll be fine. Besides, my parents will hear the car if you guys drop me off. It's not far…I'm good."

"Call me in the morning. My mom and dad are gone tomorrow for the night, so you should come stay with me."

"I will. I'll come over when I'm up and around. Michael mentioned us all going to the beach for the day, so I'll get a hold of you."

I hugged her and said goodbye to a few others and headed out the front door.

I made it to the end of the driveway when I stopped dead in my tracks by a voice I hadn't heard in awhile and a face I barely recognized in the dark night.

"I really don't think you should be walking home alone at night. It's not safe."

I turned around and saw him. Dylan McCartney.

"Dylan? What are you doing here?"

"I think the better question is what are you doing here?" he asked. "Don't you think you're a little young to be at a party drinking at almost one in the morning? And walking home alone isn't a real smart decision either."

"Wow. Nice to see you too," I sarcastically replied. "And not that it's your business, but I only had two drinks. I'm a big girl in case you hadn't noticed."

"Oh, I noticed. I saw you sitting inside on the stairs. Where's Michael?"

"He went home. I figured I should too. Everyone in there is getting wasted and I'm just not into it tonight." And then it dawned on me to ask, "How do you know about Michael?"

"This is a small town, Lindsey. It's not like it's a big secret. And in case you've forgotten, I see your sister at school all the time. She told me you were seeing Michael and that y'all had been together for awhile now."

"And how is my perfect sister doing anyway? Are you still in love with her?" I could tell he didn't like my tone and I think I struck an emotional nerve with him.

"Your sister is fine," he replied bitterly. "I'm not in love with your sister. We're friends. Always have been."

I felt bad because I knew he really did want to be with her at one point and she didn't feel the same way. In fact, she kind of used him. She liked the attention he gave her. Who wouldn't? He was good looking…chiseled face, always a five o'clock shadow, piercing blue eyes, and a smile that was devilish. He was charming and polite, and his sarcastic nature could drive girl crazy.

Why was I being so rude to him? I felt like he was treating me like a child. That's how he always saw me. Rachel's little sister Lindsey. I think it bothered me so much that he treated me like a child because even at the age of thirteen when I first met him I was crazy about him. At the time I guess it was a crush.

And now here he is standing here still treating me like a child. Looking at me like I'm still a girl that doesn't know how to take care of herself.

"Michael shouldn't have left you here by yourself."

"I'm not by myself. My friends are here. And he didn't leave me here," I said defending my boyfriend. "When I came back he was gone. He was helping a friend who needed a ride."

"Your story," he said as he smirked at me.

"Don't do that!" I snapped.

"What?" he asked again looking at me like the cat that ate the canary.

Why was this getting to me? Why was he getting to me?

"Goodnight, Dylan. Nice seeing you. Say hi to Rachel for me." I turned and started to walk away.

"Don't go," he called after me. "I'm sorry. I was just giving you a hard time. Why don't you stay awhile and we can talk? It would be great to catch up."

I turned and looked at him. I tried to be angry. It lasted for about two seconds. I smiled. He smiled. And I think that was the moment, the moment that changed my course, my path in life forever.

Dylan

As we talked, all I could do was stare at her. I couldn't believe this was the same girl I'd met just a few years ago. I always thought she was adorable but in a little sister kind of way. Now she was seventeen, still too young and completely off limits to this twenty-year-old, but I still couldn't take my eyes off her.

She was no longer "cute" in a girlish way. Now she was stunning, with longer hair that she wore straight instead of her natural curls and it had a blonde tone to it now instead of a mousy brown. Her eyes I knew were hazel, but hard to see in the darkness of the night. She had a single freckle on the tip of her nose that was adorable. I tried not to notice that her once scrawny body was now causing my mind, and my eyes, to wander.

We sat on the porch for what seemed like an eternity talking about college, high school, she talked about Michael and I told her about the girl I was seeing at school—Melissa. It was getting late and I told Melissa I would call her, but it would have to wait. I didn't want this to stop. Why was I so drawn to her? I knew I should walk her home and forget that I ever saw her. She was a forbidden thought that I couldn't erase from my memory. She was the little sister of one of my best friends. Rachel would crucify me if she even knew I was sitting here at two in the morning with her teenage sister, much less if she knew the thoughts I was thinking. She was beautiful and I couldn't help but let my imagination go places it shouldn't.

It was almost two o'clock but the sky was lit up like it was the middle of the day. The stars were out in full force and the moon was almost full.

"Do you ever wish on stars?"

She paused for a moment, lost in her thoughts. "I do. Michael thinks it's silly, but I believe in wishing on stars. He says I'm a dreamer and that I live in a fantasy world."

"There's nothing wrong with wishing on stars and having dreams. I hope they always come true for you."

I wanted to kiss her. The slight hint of lip gloss still on her lips, I wanted to taste it and hold her. She talked about Michael and their sometimes turbulent relationship. I suddenly hated him. How could he ever be anything but completely consumed and in love with this girl? She was beautiful, and funny, and that one little lonely freckle on the tip of her nose was just begging to be kissed.

I had to go. I had to get her home and forget that I ever saw her. I needed to forget the thought of kissing her and holding her and pretend that this entire night never happened.

"What's wrong?" she asked.

"Sorry, I guess I'm just tired," I lied. I couldn't tell her that I stopped paying attention to anything she was saying because all I could do was replay the thoughts of kissing her over and over again in my mind.

"Me too. I didn't realize it was so late."

"Let me walk you home." The second I said it I knew I was in trouble.

"If you insist." She smiled when she said it. "Apparently chivalry isn't dead after all."

"No ma'am," I stood up and reached for her hand to help her up off the porch steps. I hoped she couldn't tell I was slightly trembling and my palms were sweating.

When she stood we were just a few inches apart and I stood about a foot taller than her. I looked down at her and she glanced up at me.

"You've changed so much this past year." I couldn't stop myself from opening my stupid, unthinking mouth.

"What do you mean? I'm still just Rachel's little sister." She smirked at me and I could tell she was fishing for me to say something.

"Not so little anymore." I swiped back a piece of her bangs that had fallen across her eyes. My fingers grazed her forehead. I wanted to take her in my arms, hold her face in my hands, gently kiss her lips.

She stopped smiling. It was as if she was waiting for me to kiss her. Like she expected it.

But to her surprise, I didn't. I was a true southern gentleman.

We turned and walked the two blocks to her house in total silence. Maybe we were all talked out. Or maybe she was feeling the same thing I was feeling at the moment. I was afraid if I opened my mouth I'd say something I couldn't take back.

You're so beautiful. Can I kiss you? Can I hold you in my arms all night? Will you break up with that ridiculous boyfriend of yours and date me instead? These are the things that would spill out if I said anything at all. Besides, she was dating someone and even if she wasn't I was three years older than she and there was no way this could ever be anything at all. Rachael would kill me.

We reached her house and again she turned to me. She looked up at me and sarcastically whispered, "I would've been fine walking by myself."

"You shouldn't be alone. You should never have to be alone."

"I'm not alone. I have Michael."

"Michael's not here now." I replied as I took a step closer leaving just inches between us.

It was October and the night air had a chill. It was hard to tell in that moment if it was the weather or the proximity of our bodies that made her slightly tremble.

I touched her arm and asked, "Are you cold? You're shaking."

"No. I'm not cold."

I knew if I didn't kiss her now I would regret it for the rest of my life. I reached up and touched her face. She lifted her head and I pulled her toward me. I let my lips graze hers. I pulled away and our eyes locked.

"Why did you stop?" she whispered.

"Michael. Melissa. We shouldn't do this."

"I've always imagined what it would be like to be kissed by you."

Should I tell her that I felt the same way? Should I tell her that from the moment I laid eyes on her tonight and realized that she was no longer the young girl I once knew that I wanted to take her in my arms and kiss her all night? I wanted to kiss her and hold her and make her see that she deserves so much more than what she has with Michael. He doesn't deserve her.

"Well, I guess I shouldn't keep you waiting any longer." I smiled at her, and as my hands held her face I kissed her.

I didn't want to stop. I was afraid to let go of her. But I knew this was wrong. We were both involved with other people and I shouldn't be complicating things for her.

11

"I need to go. You need to go." I gently kissed her on that single freckle on her nose, then on her cheek, and whispered in her ear, "Be happy."

"So you're just going to walk away? After that…" She looked at me with those beautiful eyes. She seemed hurt and confused.

"This isn't right. We have other people that could get hurt by this. Including you. The last thing I would ever want to do is hurt you."

I turned and walked away. It was the hardest thing I'd ever done. I fought every urge to turn around and go back to her. I could feel her still standing there waiting for me to change my mind and come back. But I didn't. It wouldn't be right. It wouldn't be fair to Melissa, or Michael, and especially to Lindsey. I had a life at college, one that didn't include a seventeen-year-old junior in high school. No matter how I felt, it didn't matter.

Once at my truck again, I just sat in silence thinking. What the hell just happened? I needed to forget about anything I was feeling and get back to school. Back to where I belonged.

Melissa

So, as usual, here I sit waiting to hear from Dylan. Imagine that. When will I ever learn? Or when will he ever learn? I knew when I met him that he wasn't the kind of guy to settle down, so why did I let myself fall for him? Clearly I know why. He's charming, gorgeous, and so romantic…when he wants to be.

But once again, he's MIA. I'm still not sure why he felt the need to go home for the weekend. Homecoming weekend at your old high school shouldn't be a big deal, but try telling Dylan and his old friends that. They were all meeting back home for the weekend to go to the big game and hit a few parties afterwards.

I shouldn't have argued with him before he left. I wanted to go with him. I figured after three months of dating he might want me to meet his mom, his brother, and maybe some of his old friends from back home. That led into the inevitable fight about where our relationship is going. He wants to "take it slow…see where it goes." I, on the other hand, would like to fast forward to our one year anniversary, moving in together, getting engaged, getting married, having three kids and a dog, and…

I tend to move quickly. He drags his feet on everything.

It's now almost one in the morning and I think I've checked my cell phone forty-two times since eleven and still no call.

As I lie here trying to sleep I'm wondering what he's doing. Who is he with? It's driving me crazy!

Just as I start to doze off my phones buzzes on vibrate on the nightstand. I practically fall out of bed trying to get to it. Hoping it's him I check the brightly lit screen. Sheer disappointment. It's Shelly, my roommate.

"Where are you and when do I need to come get you?"

"Well hello to you too," she slurred.

"Shell, where are you?"

"Tavern. Can you come pick me up?"

Shelly had a tendency to overindulge, but she always called me for a ride. She knew I would be sitting home waiting for Dylan. I was always waiting for Dylan.

"I'll be there in ten."

As I drive the six miles across town to her favorite bar, I pass his house that he shares with three roommates and again all I can think of is him.

Shelly stumbles out of the bar and practically falls into the passenger seat of my car.

"What would I do without you?" she slurs.

I laughed, "Lucky for you, you'll never have to find out."

"Did I wake you up? You look like hell...what's wrong?"

Defensively I reply, "Why do you say that?!?! I'm fine. I was studying all night for my chem lab." I'm not a good liar and Shelly will see right through this ridiculous story I'm telling.

"What's the problem? Did Mr. Wonderful blow you off again tonight? I don't know what the hell you see in him anyway. He treats you like shit and yet you don't seem to care."

"He didn't blow me off!" I rebutted. "He went home this weekend to see his mom and some friends. They were all meeting back home for the homecoming game."

"Then why aren't you with him?"

"It's a 'guy thing'," I replied with sarcastic air quotes.

"When will you see that you're clearly more into him than he is to you?"

I didn't reply. We just drove the rest of the way in silence. She was in and out from all the alcohol she had clearly consumed. Once we got back to the apartment, she stumbled into her bedroom. Like the good friend that I am, I followed with a Gatorade, three Advil, and the plastic trash bucket just in case it was one of those nights. I woke her up enough to get her to take the Advil and a few swigs of the Gatorade. Then, with a few incomprehensible murmurs and a quiet, "Thank you," she passed out.

Once again, I was left alone with my thoughts racing.

I checked my phone one last time and still nothing from Dylan. I didn't want to believe the things that Shelly had been saying that maybe I was more into this relationship than he was.

When we met three months ago I was instantly attracted to him. Who wouldn't be? He's charming and absolutely gorgeous. He's got an arrogant and sarcastic sense of humor that most women find undeniably sexy. He has a reputation of being a "player" but somehow he's managed to settle into a relationship with me. Well, I guess he's as settled as he can be.

Maybe Shelly's right about him. I've been pushing to take our relationship to the next level, and he's content to stay the way we are. We're exclusive and we aren't seeing other people, but he's just not ready for things like meeting each other's family or talking about moving in together.

I must've dozed off because I was startled when my phone vibrated on the nightstand. It's him…finally. Almost three in the morning.

"Sorry it's so late. Just got home from a party." He sounded like he was fulfilling his duty to call me instead of being genuinely apologetic.

"That must've been quite a party." I'm certain he could hear the pissed off tone of my voice. "It's almost 3:00 A.M."

Obviously he wasn't in the mood for an argument or to hear his girlfriend complaining. "I'm not going to do this with you tonight, Melissa. I'll call you tomorrow."

"Fine. Goodnight." As I hung up the phone I was furious for sitting home waiting for him all night. I should be out having fun…having a life.

Typical Dylan. I guess it's better than nothing. At least he remembered to call this time. Most of the time he forgets and I hear from him the next day. Shelly says I should expect more, and that I deserve better. But I love him. And someday hopefully he'll love me.

Lindsey

When I woke up the next morning all I could think about was that kiss. I couldn't believe after all those years of knowing him that suddenly things have changed. I never would've dreamed anything like that would have happened. I had always wished for it, but I never imagined in a million years I would have been standing there kissing him last night. Now what? What the hell was I supposed to tell my boyfriend? And my sister? Oh God, if Rachel found out she would kill me. There's no way this even matters. It's Dylan. He's a player. He has a girlfriend back at school. It probably meant nothing to him. Things will just continue on the way they were before last night. No one would even have to know. He'll go back to school and things will just continue here the way they were before he came back.

I hadn't even noticed that my phone was ringing. I was so lost in my own thoughts that I had no idea what was going on around me. How in the world did I miss three calls? I checked the caller ID…Michael, of course. No voice-mails. So I picked up the phone and called him back.

"Where the hell have you been? I've called you three times!"

He was angry. This was going to be a long day.

"I was sleeping. I'm sorry."

"Are we still going to the beach today or what?"

"Of course. Why wouldn't we?" Did I sound guilty? I'm acting like I have something to hide. I did nothing wrong. It was one kiss. Dylan and I are friends. I've known him for years. It was just an innocent kiss. It'll never happen again.

"Hello? Seriously, what's going on with you? First you don't answer your phone all morning and then when you finally call me back it's like you're in left field."

"Sorry, I guess I'm just tired," I lied.

"Well, how late did you stay last night?"

For some reason I wanted to lie to him like I had something to hide. Honestly, I don't even remember what time I left the party. I said goodbye to everyone, but when I left I ran into Dylan. I don't know how long we sat outside and talked or what time it was when I finally got home.

"I left around one." I knew that was the truth. It just wasn't all of the truth.

He wasn't buying it. "You didn't call me to tell me you were home."

"I watched TV when I got home and forgot to call you until I was almost asleep. I figured by then you would be sleeping and I didn't want to wake you." He would see right through that answer. I never did anything without calling him every half hour.

"Since when do you forget to call me? Something's not right. Chad said you left at one and you should've called me when you got home."

Michael liked to know where I was at all times, even though the same didn't go for letting me know his whereabouts. I was partly to blame for it because I had always reported in to him as if he was my keeper.

He was getting angry. He had a really bad temper. The last thing I wanted to do was fight with him. Lately he had gotten worse, and last month he grabbed my arm during a fight and left a bruise on my wrist. He didn't mean to, and he apologized later when he realized that he'd hurt me.

"Nothing's going on. You went home. You left knowing I would be back. I didn't think you'd give a shit about what time I got home. You didn't bother to come back even though you knew I'd be there." I was pushing his buttons. Picking a fight with him wasn't a good idea. It wouldn't end well. It never did.

"I told the guys to keep an eye on you. I should've made one of them drive you home."

"I'm not a child, Michael! I don't need a babysitter!" Now I was yelling at him. I was getting defensive. He always treats me like I'm a piece of property to him.

It would be smart at this point if I just changed the subject or apologized to him. He would make the rest of the day miserable if I didn't.

"You're not a child, but you're MY girlfriend! I want to know where you are!"

Normally I would pacify him, but for some reason I was agitating him and I didn't care.

"Well, maybe if you were so concerned with what I was doing and where I was, you would've stuck around to pay attention! Maybe if I was as important to you as your friends you'd know where I was and what I was doing!" I was pissed. Relationships shouldn't be about one person keeping tabs on the other.

"What the hell has gotten into you? I don't need this crap from you." He hung up.

Oh God, what have I done? I should know better by now than to make him angry. I tried calling him back several times but he didn't answer.

I lay in bed for an hour trying to call to apologize. That's all I ever do… apologize. Even if I haven't done anything wrong…I apologize. We go around and around in circles like this all the time. It makes my head dizzy. I try so hard to keep him happy.

I closed my eyes and I must've fallen asleep because the next thing I know I woke up and there he was. Not Michael…Dylan.

"What the hell are you doing here?!?! How did you get into my house?"

"Wow. Great to see you too," he was smirking. "You look awful."

"Geez, thanks a lot. And don't change the subject. How the hell did you get in my house?"

"Have you forgotten that your sister and I were best friends all through high school? I've snuck her in and out of this house a couple dozen times over the years. I know where the key is hidden."

I was happy to see him. "Well, you could've knocked…or called." I smiled. I really was happy to see him.

We sat in silence for a few minutes. What the hell is he doing here? If Michael were here he would be furious. He would accuse me of all sorts of things. He gets crazy jealous when guys even talk to me. If he knew Dylan was here in my house, inches from my bed, he would lose his mind.

He just kept staring at me. "What's wrong" he asked.

"Why do you think something's wrong?" It was as if he could read my thoughts. He knew something was going on. "You can't be here." I kept looking out the window scared to death that Michael would come by and see his truck here. That would be the last thing I needed right now.

"Why not? Are you expecting someone else?" He was grinning. He knew what I meant.

"If Michael sees your truck in in the driveway he'll think there's something going on."

"Well, isn't there?"

"Isn't there what?" I started feeling like the room was spinning. Suddenly it felt like it was a hundred degrees in my room. "I don't know what you're talking about."

"Come on," he reached his hand out to help me out of bed. "Let's get you to a doctor."

"What? What are you talking about?"

He laughed, "Clearly there's something wrong with you. You're shaking, and you look like you're going to pass out. You're about to tear a hole in your bottom lip if you don't stop biting it. And you obviously have fallen and hit your head and are experiencing some sort of amnesia because you don't re-member this…"

He was holding the side of my face in both of his hands, and pulled me toward him and kissed me again. I knew I should push him away, but it was as if my arms wouldn't work anymore. The world just stopped for a few moments. He was right. I was shaking, and the room felt like it was spinning. What the hell is he doing to me? I can't do this. I can't do this. But I couldn't stop kissing him. I didn't want to stop. My world as I knew it was about to change com-pletely. I had to get him out of here but I couldn't let him go.

Finally I pushed him away. He looked at me half confused and half hurt. I could tell that this was not just a game to him. Is it possible that he really has feelings for me? Or is he just that good at playing the game and I'm just that naïve that I can't tell the difference? Right now the answer to that question didn't matter. Getting him out of my house mattered more. If Michael showed up here things would get out of control.

"Please stop. You have to leave," I was pleading with him now. The last thing I wanted was for him to have to deal with what was going to happen if my boyfriend showed up here. I knew how to handle him, but there was no reason to drag someone else into my mess of a relationship. I cared too much about Dylan to let that happen. He didn't need this chaos in his life. He should go back to school and forget about this. Forget about me.

"I'm sorry. I thought you felt something last night between us. I did. I couldn't leave without seeing you. I wanted to know if last night meant any-thing to you at all."

The words that came out of my mouth weren't mine. They didn't come from my heart. This is exactly what I had wanted for as long as I can remember. But I wanted to save him from the backlash and the fallout...so I lied.

"I didn't. I didn't feel anything. I'm sorry if you read into it, but that kiss never should've happened. You should have never come here this morning. Go back to college, Dylan. There's nothing here for you. I love Michael. He'll be here any minute so you need to leave."

I felt sick. My heart was breaking. I wanted to wrap my arms around him and bury my face in his chest and tell him to never leave me. But he had a life at school, and I wasn't a part of it. He needed to see where that would take him.

He was hurt. I could see it all over his face. Could he tell I was lying to him? I wanted to tell him how I really felt. I was scared. Scared of Michael. Scared of Dylan. Dylan could take my heart, tie it into knots, and crush it. I needed to protect myself, and him, so I lied.

A tear slid down my cheek. Please, Dylan, please leave before I beg you to stay.

"I'm sorry. I didn't mean to upset you. That's the last thing I would ever want to do." He grabbed my hand. He kissed it. Then he leaned in and kissed the single freckle on the end of my nose. "Be happy, short stack."

And there it was...the name that would forever take me back to being his best friend's little sister..."short stack." He and Rachel used to call me that when I would constantly tag along with them to the mall. I used to hate that name, but now it was making my heart melt.

Then he turned and walked out. I had no idea when I would ever see him again. I wanted to chase after him and tell him I lied. I wanted to tell him that I did feel something. I felt something so strong that I cared enough about him to let him walk out that door. I had no idea he could ever feel that way about me though. I buried my head in the pillow, and I cried.

I wondered how I would ever be able to forget about him and what happened last night. This was the guy that I had fantasized about being with for years. I dreamed of what it would be like to kiss him and now that it had happened I couldn't just erase the memory. His life was back in College Station and mine was here. I couldn't be a part of his world. There was no room in it for me.

Michael

Something isn't right. Lindsey doesn't act like this, and it's not like her to 'forget' to call me. I should've never left Chad's house. If I would've gone back then everything would be fine. We'd be on our way to the beach for a great Saturday with our friends.

"Hey Mike, where's Lindsey?" asked Mac. "I thought we were picking her and Keri up then heading to the beach?"

"I don't know what her problem is today. Something's going on. She's acting like a bitch and she left the party at one, but I never heard from her when she got home."

"I saw her leave around one. We all kept an eye on her just like you asked. She was alone when she left. What was her excuse for not getting a hold of you when she got home?"

"She said she was just watching TV and forgot."

Mac laughed and said, "Doesn't seem like her at all. Especially since she won't leave you alone long enough for you to take a piss without her calling."

"She keeps calling and I just don't feel like dealing with her shit today. Let's just go and I'll deal with her later."

I knew he was right and that there was more to this than Lindsey was telling me. My phone vibrated again…fifth time in a half hour. She's relentless.

"If you don't answer she'll just keep calling."

I was still too mad to talk to her. She was hiding something from me and I wanted to make her sweat it out for awhile. I hit ignore on my phone and put it in my pocket. "Let's go."

We loaded up the truck with chairs, a cooler, and other beach necessities and headed out. Mac called Keri before we left and told her we were on our way. She hadn't heard from Lindsey yet today, which was also strange. They did everything together and were rarely apart.

We showed up at Keri's house a few minutes later.

"Aren't we picking up Lindsey?"

I knew Keri was going to insist that we stop and pick Lindsey up. "Nope, I'm not in the mood for it today."

Keri looked surprised, "But last night she said she planned on going with us today? Let me just call her and see what's going on. She's going to be pissed if we go without her."

"Whatever. I don't care. Something's not right with her today. Did something happen last night at the party after I left?"

"No, she just got tired and said she wasn't in the mood to stay all night. I offered to get her a ride home but she insisted that she was fine to walk alone. I haven't heard from her this morning which is weird because I told her to call me so we could make plans for her to stay with me tonight." Keri looked worried. "Do you think something happened to her?"

"I don't know, but she wasn't acting like herself today on the phone, and she never called me when she got home last night. That's not like her at all."

Lindsey answered and told Keri she wasn't sure if she was coming with us. She didn't say, but I'm sure Lindsey told Keri that we had argued.

Keri hung up the phone, clearly uncomfortable. "Let's just stop and get her. She's going to be upset if we don't, and I'll never hear the end of it. Besides, I'll be bored to death while you guys do your thing all day if she's not there."

"Fine. We can get her. Tell her to be ready in five because I'm not waiting."

Lindsey

I felt horrible about what happened with Michael this morning. Even worse about what I did to Dylan. I needed to forget about that for now though. Michael, Mac, and Keri were on their way to pick me up and if I wasn't ready when Michael got here it would only make things worse than they already were today. Michael didn't like to be kept waiting, and today his patience would be at an all-time low. So I hurried into my bikini, grabbed a towel, my phone, some sunscreen, left a note for my parents, and headed out the door just as they were pulling in the driveway. I climbed in the backseat with Keri. Michael was silent. I knew he was still angry with me, and I wasn't going to push it with him.

Once we got to the beach, things fell into our typical Saturday routine. There were a half dozen of the guys from the football team there with their girlfriends, music playing from the speakers in someone's truck, all of us girls on our towels baking in the sun while the guys threw around a football. It was like any other Saturday we'd spent a hundred times before.

I was losing my mind over what happened last night and just an hour ago with Dylan. My thoughts were spinning and I felt like I was slipping in and out of the present. The girls were all talking about the dance last night and the party at Chad's, but I was lost in my own preoccupied mind.

I asked Keri if she wanted to go for a walk. I felt like if I didn't tell someone what was going on in my mind I would explode. Besides, Keri would be the voice of reason and tell me that what happened with Dylan was insignificant and she'd convince me to forget about it. Always my voice of reason when my imagination got the best of me, Keri was truly my best friend. She knew everything about me.

We got about fifty feet down the beach and away from the others and she could tell something was bothering me.

"Ok, spill it. What's going on with you? You've barely said a word since we picked you up. Clearly you and Michael had a fight, but that's nothing new. You always call me first thing in the morning and I never heard from you. You're a million miles away in that cute little head of yours and I want to know why."

"Am I that transparent?" I laughed.

"Yes, you are." She smiled. "But it's not about a fight with Michael. You two fight so much that it's not normal when you're getting along. It's something else, and you better start talking."

"Something happened when I left Chad's house last night."

She looked horrified and on the verge of tears. "Oh my god, what happened? Did someone hurt you? Are your parents fighting again? Don't tell me your stepdad left this time?"

"No, it's not my parents. Honestly, I don't know where they are this weekend."

That was a subject for an entirely different day. Since my stepdad's job had been downsized things had gotten tense in the house and I was certain that at anytime they would be splitting. They fought constantly and he spent a lot of nights on the couch these days.

"Then what's going on? You're scaring me."

"I'm fine. Physically anyway. When I started walking home last night I ran into someone. Dylan."

Keri looked confused at first. "McCartney? Where did you run into him?"

"He stopped me as I was leaving the party. We sat on the porch and drank a few beers and talked for about an hour."

"Well, that explains why you never called Michael when you got home. Does he know you were with Dylan?"

"NO! You know what he would do if I was even talking to another guy inside the house where his buddies could keep an eye on me, so let's not even think about how pissed he'd be if he knew I was alone with a guy talking and drinking a few beers!"

"So tell me how you ended up sitting on the porch drinking beer with Dylan? That's random. What was he doing there?"

"He was stopping at the party I guess. He saw me leaving and asked me to sit and have a beer with him. I didn't know what to do. You know how I feel about him."

"I do. And that's what makes me nervous about hearing where this story is going. What did you two talk about?"

"Just random stuff, Michael, his girlfriend Melissa, college, high school… I don't know, we just talked." I knew I had to tell her the rest. I was hesitating though. It wasn't that I didn't trust her. I trusted Keri with my life. I just didn't know how to even process how I felt about what happened. "He insisted on walking me home."

Again, I was stalling. We had reached a spot on the beach away from the group and sat down on some driftwood near the docks. I circled my toes in the sand and could feel the heat rising inside me as I tried to finish telling Keri what happened. Suddenly I realized there were tears rolling down my sun-burned cheeks and I couldn't hide what I was feeling.

"He kissed me."

"Oh, wow."

She put her arms around me and as my emotions poured out I sobbed.

"Michael doesn't have to know. It was just a kiss, Linds. Let it go. If you're worried about him finding out, I promise he won't hear it from me."

"Honestly, that's not what's bothering me. Keri, I've wanted Dylan to see me as something other than Rachel's little sister since the day I met him. And now that he did, I pushed him away. I told him to leave, and it killed me inside. I know it hurt him too. He came back this morning."

"He came to your house?"

"I woke up and he was in my bedroom. He wanted me to say that the kiss meant something, and I lied. I told him that it meant nothing to me and that he should go back to college."

"What did he do?"

"He left. His kissed me, told me to be happy and he walked away. I wanted to tell him to stay. You know I've fantasized about this since I can remember. But it doesn't make sense for us to even consider where something could go between us. I mean, he's in college with a girlfriend and I'm in high school with a boyfriend."

"I know, Linds, but this is Dylan we're talking about. The guy whose last name you used to write with your first name just to see how it would sound when you married him someday." She laughed and as I wiped the tears from my eyes I finally laughed too. "It must've killed you to turn him away."

"You know how I feel about Michael. If I didn't love him so much I wouldn't stay in this relationship. I don't want to ruin what I have with him."

"Your relationship with Michael is based on convenience and you know it. That's all it is. People expect you to be together because it works. But you don't love him."

Keri knew me better than I knew myself sometimes. She never sugarcoated how she felt about anything, and my relationship with Michael was no different. It wasn't that she didn't like Michael, but she was like a sister to me and she knew that he didn't always treat me the way he should.

I thought about what she said. Do I really love him or do I love the idea of 'Michael and Lindsey?' I looked down the beach where he was throwing a football with the other guys. It was the picture perfect group of people. The guys were teammates and friends and their girlfriends were cheerleaders and followed the guys wherever they went. What if she was right? What if I was just with him because it was easy and because it was what was expected from the captain of the football team and his trophy cheerleader girlfriend. Regardless of how things were with Michael, the idea of Dylan and me wasn't something to even consider. We live in two different worlds. And that's where we would stay, for now, maybe always.

Dylan

I don't know what the hell just happened, but clearly I misread what was going on last night between Linds and I. When did she become so beautiful? And had she always been such a pain in the ass? Yeah, definitely.

I never looked at her like I did last night. She's always been like a little sister to me. Oh God, that's awful! I must be completely out of my mind to think that there could've been something between us last night…or ever.

For starters, Rachel would absolutely forbid it. She'd crucify me for even speaking to her baby sister, and if she knew even the half of what went through my mind last night she would kill me herself.

And what about Melissa? She didn't sound happy at all with my 3 A.M. phone call last night. I'm such an idiot for thinking she wouldn't be pissed about not being invited back home with me for the weekend. She's been pushing me to meet my mom, my brother, and my friends from back home and I keep putting her off. She's great and I really like being with her, but I'm just not ready for that yet. Commitment like that scares the hell out of me.

Last night I don't know what possessed me to kiss Lindsey. I thought there was some sort of connection between us while we were sitting there talking. When I touched her hand to help her up off the steps I thought I felt something pass between us. It sounds ridiculous now. Clearly she doesn't feel anything like I did. I don't understand why she pushed me away this morning. Maybe it's Michael, and she's feeling guilty about the kiss. Apparently she hasn't heard the things about Michael that I've heard. Michael is a complete ass to her. That arrogant son of a bitch has been screwing around on her for months. How can she be so blind to not see it? Rachel has been hearing from several friends still in the area that Michael's seeing a girl from our neighboring school and Lindsey is completely oblivious to it. She deserves much better than what that guy can offer to her.

But who the hell am I to say? I'm no better than him. Last night I should've been home, back at school, and instead I was kissing a girl I had no business being with while my girlfriend sat at home three hours away most likely staring at her phone all night waiting for me to call. Now who's the ass?

I certainly wouldn't be the one to tell Lindsey about Michael's infidelities. It's not fair to keep it from her, but it's not my place to tell her. She's a big girl, she can figure it out on her own. Rachel wanted to tell her, but she didn't want to break her heart. Honestly, I think she'd be doing her a favor.

Last night he probably left the party to go to some girl's house while poor Lindsey risked getting in trouble to go back and see him only to find him gone already. And of course his buddies would cover for him and then watch her like it was their job. Maybe they saw us together out on the front porch drinking and laughing. That would be poetic justice for him to get a taste of what he'd been doing to her for months.

None of this is my business because she isn't anyone to me. She's my friend's sister, and that's all. Time to pack my things and head back to my world. My world where teenage girls, homecoming parties, and small-town drama doesn't exist. I'll apologize to Melissa and try to start making this thing with her work, whatever it is. Lindsey can take care of herself. She doesn't need me here. She told me herself that she felt nothing, so as far as I'm concerned last night and this morning didn't happen.

I called Melissa and told her I'd be back earlier than expected. She seemed happy and surprised, and something in me was glad that I was going back to her…back to where I belonged.

It was wrong for me to think that showing up in Lindsey's bedroom this morning was a good idea. What was I thinking? She's a teenage girl who doesn't need any more drama in her life to make things harder on her. It's bad enough that her parents are in such turmoil, and her boyfriend is cheating on her. Me being a part of her life now would only be adding fuel to the fire. Regardless, she has plenty of people here to help her through all of her troubles, so clearly she doesn't need another problem in her life. She doesn't need me.

I said goodbye to my mother who was more than disappointed that I wouldn't be staying for dinner and catching part of the football game with her. My mother and I had a tradition of sorts to spend Sunday afternoons watching the Houston Astros and cooking steaks on the grill. Today she would have to catch the game without me. I thought about telling her what happened last night with Lindsey, but she would most likely think I was crazy for doing what I did. She would tell me all the things I already knew about why kissing Lindsey was wrong. I think she understood when I told her I needed to get back. This will always be my home, but there's nothing for me here, at least for now.

Lindsey

Things just kind of seemed to keep moving along for the rest of my junior year as they normally did. Michael and I kept up our routine of fighting and making up and being the "class couple" that everyone envied. Such a picture perfect scene from the outside looking in. Underneath was ugly though, and keeping the secrets of our troubled relationship was taking its toll on me.

Michael became increasingly jealous and overprotective throughout the year and I felt as though he was suffocating me. We would never go anywhere without each other. Well, at least I wouldn't be able to go without him, but he always did his own thing whenever he wanted to. If I tried to question him it just made things worse. He started hanging out with a few guys from another school and would sometimes go to their parties and would always tell me that it was just the guys and I wasn't allowed to come.

My family was unravelling slowly over the past year or so, and from day to day I wasn't sure what to expect. Rachel stopped coming home much at all because the atmosphere was so tense and uncomfortable.

I started spending any and all of my free time at Keri's house to get away from what was happening at home. Keri's family took me in as one of them. Her parents were so sweet and loving. Keri's "mama" as we called her would make us a full breakfast every morning complete with pancakes, bacon, eggs, and home fries. It didn't matter if it was a hectic weekday morning or a peaceful Sunday. She was always in her robe in the kitchen making a feast for us all. She would always pour us these little glasses of orange juice as we sat at the breakfast bar waiting to be served. She packed lunches for all of us and kissed us all goodbye as we headed to school. I spent every weekend with them and many weeknights as well. Keri's dad bought a trundle bed for me to sleep on in her room and we shared a closet and bathroom. She was like a sister to me.

My brother had moved back to our father's house in New York State a few months ago, and without Rachel at home I couldn't handle being the only child in the house with all of the fighting between my mother and my stepdad. I knew it was inevitable that eventually my stepdad would be gone and it would just be my mom and me. I wasn't sure what that meant for me, but I just knew that things would never be the same. Lately every time I came home I never knew what to expect. Most of the time I just got more clothes and left. My house no longer felt like my home. I'm sure my mother missed me, but she was consumed with the downfall of her marriage. The last thing she needed was her teenage daughter and all of the drama that came along with my life.

That summer after our junior year, I stayed busy with my summer job hostessing at a local restaurant, spending days off at the beach with Michael, Keri, and the "gang", and riding the merry-go-round of a relationship with Michael.

I heard the rumors about Michael that everyone was talking about. His infidelity seemed to be the talk of the town lately and I tried to ignore the things I kept hearing but it was starting to take a toll on me. I knew I would have to confront Michael and find out the truth for myself.

This weekend was the last one before our senior year. We all rented a beach house in Galveston to have one last hoorah before it began. Our final year. I was determined to make this year different. I wanted to start being Lindsey without Michael for a change. He had plenty of time to himself and I felt trapped and isolated from people because of the hold he had on me.

I decided this would be a good opportunity for me to talk to him about the rumors I'd been hearing and maybe give our relationship a different direction. I wanted to know who I was without him. My entire high school years were all about him. I wanted my senior year to be about me. My dreams, my goals, my interests, and my decisions.

The first day at the beach house was spent like a typical day with our group. The girls lay in the sun on the beach gossiping about anything and everything, slathering ourselves with baby oil trying to achieve the perfect tan, watching the guys while they threw the football around and did a little surfing.

Late in the afternoon we headed back to the house for pizza, naps, and showers. Once it was dark we started the bonfire on the beach and settled in for the night. Couples huddled under blankets while the radio played and we all traded stories about our summer, senior year expectations, and plans for after graduation in May.

Most of us had already applied to colleges. Keri and Mac had already both taken early acceptance scholarships with Baylor University, Keri for academics and Mac for football. Trisha was planning to go to University of Texas in Austin and Chris was still undecided about UT or SWTSU. Southwest Texas State University was only about forty-five minutes from Austin and that was most likely where he was headed. Michael had been offered football scholarships from SMU, Texas Tech, and Texas A&M. His father and older brother, both alumni of Southern Methodist University, had hoped that he would choose SMU, but Michael wanted to do his own thing. He was leaning toward A&M and of course wanted me to do the same.

Unfortunately, the current situation of my mother and stepdad and their inevitable divorce would most likely make A&M financially unattainable for me. I had applied for a couple scholarships but it wouldn't be enough even if I got both of them. And honestly, I wanted to do my own thing. I was considering staying in Katy and going to University of Houston so I could work and help pay for school. Keri's parents had sat me down and talked about my situation at home and they graciously offered to let me move in with them once Keri left for Baylor. I practically lived with them anyway so it wouldn't change much for any of us. They told me that it would make them miss Keri less if I was there, but I really knew that they were doing it because I was like one of their own. They never made me feel like a charity case. And I never took advantage of their generosity. I carried my weight in the household. Chores were evenly divided amongst myself, Keri, and her brother Walker and I always tried to do more than my share.

We were all talking about our upcoming senior year and soon everyone was talking about plans for after graduation, a subject I really wanted to avoid for now.

"So Linds, have you heard anything back from A&M yet?"

I glared at Mac when he asked because he knew this was a sore topic of conversation for me. He had been with Keri and I one night this summer after a horrible fight between Michael and I about colleges and what we'd be doing after high school. Michael just expected me to follow him wherever he went and I had other plans. I love Michael. I have never known anything but loving him. And that's exactly why I knew I had to figure out who I was without being with him every day.

"Actually yes, I did hear from them."

"And? Well, don't keep us in suspense," he said.

I didn't want to have this conversation with everyone, just with Michael. Although it might be easier with everyone here. Keri and Trisha were my closest friends and they knew things weren't good with Michael anymore. I suspect they both believed the rumors about his cheating because neither of them tried to talk me out of believing the stories.

"I got my acceptance letter."

They all cheered. I was the only one that didn't.

"Linds, why didn't you tell me?" Michael looked hurt and a little angry at the same time. "I can't believe you haven't said anything about it. All this time I kept thinking maybe you didn't get in or didn't get the scholarships you applied for so I didn't bring it up."

"Well, I got the acceptance and the scholarships but I've been waiting to hear from a couple other schools too."

He looked bewildered. I know in his mind it was a no-brainer and I would just follow him wherever he decided to go. It never occurred to him that I may have plans that didn't include him.

"What do you mean other schools? I didn't know you applied anywhere else."

Now his tone had switched from surprised and confused to angered and irritated. Typical Michael. This is always where it went. Anytime I had a thought of my own that didn't completely coincide with his thoughts it was an argument. If I disagreed with him, it was an argument. If I challenged him on anything or questioned him on anything, an argument.

"I decided to apply at a few other schools in case things didn't work out with A&M."

"Why wouldn't things work out?"

It's like he has no idea about anyone's life except his own. He's oblivious to the fact that my family was in shambles and that unlike his, my parents didn't come from money. We weren't low class or poor, but we were a typical, middle-class, working family. And now that family was crumbling and my mom was a single mom, my stepdad was moving to San Antonio, and my real dad who I felt like I barely knew was sixteen hundred miles away in New York raising my brother and a new family of his own. He had spent the last few years footing the bill for Rachel at Texas A&M with the understanding that my mother and her husband would be paying for my four years of college. Obviously that wasn't going to happen now, so it was up to me to take out the loans, apply for the grants and scholarships and hope for the best. But I wasn't willing to take on an enormous amount of debt just to follow Michael to A&M, especially with all of the cheating rumors which at this point I believed to be true.

"Well, Michael in case you hadn't noticed my family has fallen apart. My stepdad who was supposed to pay for my college has left my mother. And my father has his new family to pay for and he is stuck paying for Rachel's four years of college. There's nothing left for me. It's all on me to pay for it if I want to go to school. And honestly, I don't know if that's what I really want anyway. It's what YOU want, Michael, not me. I've followed you around for three years. What makes you think I want to keep following? Maybe, just maybe, I'd like to find my own way for a change. I'd like to make decisions that I want instead of always going along with what you want. I want to have a life of my own."

Everyone was silent. It was like waiting for a bomb to explode. Instead of the ticking timer, the only sound was the waves coming in and hitting the shoreline and the faint tone of the radio.

Michael was taken back by my blunt answer. I never challenged him or raised my voice. I guess it was a combination of his complete lack of comprehension that my life at home had completely turned upside down and the fact that my gut instinct was telling me all summer, and recently I had seen for myself, he was seeing someone behind my back that made me snap. Immediately I thought, *What the hell have I just done?*

He stared at me silently for what felt like hours until his blank stare turned to pure disdain. He glared at me. I was waiting for it. I knew what was coming. This was going to be unlike any of our fights before. I all but said that I was breaking up with him. Is that what I was doing? Maybe it was.

"Are you fucking kidding me, Lindsey? You wait until now to dump this on me?"

"Dump this on YOU?" I was not going to back down now. He was not going to make this my fault. Not this time. "How in the hell can you sit there and say I'm dumping something on you? Where the hell have you been for the last year while my life was falling apart? Oh wait, I know. You've been out screwing around for the past year!"

He looked like he was going to explode. But instead he just laughed. "You don't know what you're talking about. You're being ridiculous."

"I'm being ridiculous? Are you seriously going to sit here and deny it Michael? Everyone here knows you've been screwing that slut Leslie from Sugarland." I turned to Mac and Chris, "Come on guys, you don't have to lie for him anymore. His secret is out."

Everyone just sat in silence staring at us, completely unsure of what to do or say.

"Lindsey, shut up! Just shut the fuck up! What are you going to do, break up with me?" he laughed.

"Actually, that sounds like the best idea I've heard in a long long time." I stood and turned to head toward the beach house. I got about two steps and he grabbed my arm.

"Linds, wait!" His tone had gone from angry to desperate. "Lindsey, just hear me out. I'm sorry. It's not what you think. It's over. It's been over for awhile."

"Really, Michael? I saw you with her. Two days ago I saw the two of you."

"I'll end it, I promise. She doesn't mean anything to me. I love you. You know I love you."

"If you love me then why the hell did you start screwing around with her?"

"It was a mistake," he pleaded. "A stupid, horrible mistake. You have to believe me that I'll end it with her for good. Please, let's just work this out and I promise it'll never happen again."

"I'm going home. I need to be alone. I need to think."

"Wait, don't leave. We can stay here and talk this out."

I wanted to run away and never look back. "No Michael, I just want to get the hell out of here. Just let me go." I pulled my arm from his grasp and turned to leave.

And that's when things changed forever.

"No!" he shouted and grabbed me by the back of my hair. He threw me to the ground and before I knew what was happening his hands were around my throat and I couldn't breathe. I tried to scream but nothing would come out. He had me pinned to the ground with all of his weight on my torso and

38

his hands were choking me. He was almost twice my size and a strong athlete. I was terrified. This person who claimed to love me and was pleading with me not to leave him was doing the unthinkable.

It felt like an eternity but thankfully it was only a few seconds before Mac pulled him off of me.

"What the hell are you doing?" he screamed at Michael.

Michael just stood there staring at me. Keri and Trisha rushed to my side to make sure I was alright. I was shaking and trying to catch my breath.

Mac shoved Michael as if trying to snap him out of the daze he was in.

Chris yelled at him and they both dragged him away from where I was still laying on the ground.

"Are you okay?" Keri was crying now and Trisha had gone up to the house to get me some water.

"I'm fine, I guess. I don't know. What just happened?"

"Has he ever done that to you before?"

"No. Never." I was in shock. Michael was arrogant and cocky but he was never aggressive with me. I had never been scared of him, at least not until this moment.

Keri was helping me up, as I was still dazed and shocked about what just happened. "Come on, Linds, let's go."

I got to my feet, now in tears, and walked through the sand to the beach house. Once we got to the house, Trisha came at me with a million questions and hovering.

"Stop. Just stop!" I was breaking down. "I know you're both trying to help, but I just want to be alone. I need to get the hell out of here."

"Whatever you need," Keri backed away. "We'll help you get your things packed."

"No, I just want to leave now. I want to get as far away from him as possible right now." I picked up my keys from the counter, found my purse hanging on the back of one of the kitchen chairs, and threw a sweatshirt over my head. I went upstairs and grabbed a few things, tossed them into my bag and headed back downstairs. "I'll be fine. I'm going home."

I knew my friends were just concerned about me, but I needed to get out of there immediately.

Keri gave me a hug, "Text me when you get to your house so we know you made it okay."

I hugged them both, "I'm sorry, I love you both, but I need to be alone."

I hurried out the front door, knowing Michael would no doubt be right behind me trying to apologize once again for screwing up. This time no apology was going to fix what he had done.

Michael

I have no idea what the hell just happened. I was shaking all over, but I couldn't tell if it was anger or complete shock of what I had done. I just lost it. There's no other way to explain what I did other than that I just lost it. She pisses me off when she throws shit in my face like that. I can't believe she saw me with Leslie. Shit.

"Let go of me! What the hell?" I yanked my arms from Mac's grip and shoved him backward.

"Jesus, Mike, you were choking her! What the fuck is wrong with you? You could've hurt her!"

"I don't know. I just got so pissed and the next thing I knew I was on top of her. I never meant to hurt her. I'd never hurt Lindsey, Mac you have to believe me."

Chris had gone up to the house to check on the girls and make sure Lindsey was okay. The girls had taken her inside and I could hear her crying as they helped her up and led her to the house. I already regretted what I had done. I would never intentionally hurt her. But hadn't I already hurt her? Leslie meant nothing to me and I risked everything with Lindsey for her. And now I may have lost her for good.

"I've never seen you like that. You're lucky she isn't hurt. So what if she doesn't want to follow you to college? She's just going to tie you down anyway. You obviously didn't give a shit about her when you started fucking around with Leslie."

"Who's side are you on here Mac?"

"There's no side. You screwed up and got caught. So either move on without her or go in there and apologize and try to make this right."

Mac walked toward the house and I just stood there still trying to figure out what I had done. She was never anything but good to me and I screwed it all up. I sat down in the sand and stared at the blackness of the water.

Do I even want to make things right with her? We fight and make up like it's a daily routine. It's become such the norm for us that I don't know what it's like to not be arguing and making up every five minutes. I could walk away from her and have another one just like her tomorrow. But I don't want another one. I want her. And I don't want anyone else to have her. She's been mine since the beginning of high school and I always figured we would be together until the day we walked out of there next summer. I assumed she and I would head to A&M together, and I never gave it another thought that she wouldn't want the same thing.

I sat there alone for what felt like forever trying to figure out what to do. My body was paralyzed and searing with adrenaline. I looked down at my hands. They were trembling. How could I do that to her? She's so small and fragile and I could've broken her into pieces with my bare hands. I had to make this right.

When I got to the house everyone was sitting around the kitchen table looking distraught. The girls shot daggers at me with their eyes and I could tell they had both been crying.

"Where's Linds?" They all just stared at me and no one answered. "Is she upstairs? I need to talk to her."

"She's gone Michael. Did you really think after what you did that she'd be able to stay here with you! You could've killed her! What the hell were you thinking?"

"Stop being dramatic, Keri. He wasn't going to hurt her." Mac grabbed a couple beers and handed one in my direction.

"You cheated on her and it's her fault? I'm sorry, but explain that to me because I don't see how she did anything to deserve you choking her?" Keri was shaking and crying now. "She went home to get away from you. You need to give her some space and let her go for awhile."

"I'm going after her. I need to find her and make this right." I started to walk toward the door but Mac grabbed me and Chris stood in between me and the door. "What's your problem, guys? Let go of me. Chris, get the hell out of the way."

Chris stood his ground and at 6'4" and 220 pounds he was like a steel door in between me and the way out of the house. There are some battles that you just know you're not going to win, and this was one of them now.

"Dude, you need to calm down and give Lindsey time to chill. Besides, you've been drinking so no way are you driving." Chris was adamant and I knew there was no arguing with him or Mac for that matter.

Keri was still crying and visibly shaken. Linds was her best friend so what happened to one happened to the other. They were like sisters, joined at the hip. I knew if I had any chance of getting Lindsey to forgive me I'd have to start with her friends.

"I don't know what happened. I was just so fucking pissed that I lost it. How could she do this to me? All along I've been thinking we were going away to school together and that nothing would change."

Trisha spoke up reluctantly, "How could you think that things wouldn't change? She knew you were screwing around on her. Did you just think she would be okay with you fooling around with that slut? Have you even noticed that things aren't exactly peachy in her life right now either?"

"What are you talking about? She's never said anything to me about being unhappy." I was genuinely confused. Was I that clueless or was I just too busy doing what I wanted to do that I didn't even see what was happening with her?

"She's been practically living at my house!" Keri was crying again and now she seemed more pissed than upset. "Her parents are getting divorced and she hasn't even been staying at her own house for months. Her stepfather moved out and went to San Antonio. She's all alone, Michael. Rachel is at school and her brother was shipped back to New York with her real dad. Now she has no one and she has no idea what's next for her. So you'll have to excuse her if she doesn't give a shit about following you to A&M because she probably won't even be able to go to college because she has no idea what the fuck she's even going to be doing next week much less next year!"

"I—I didn't know it was that bad." I felt like a complete ass. My girlfriend's life was completely turning upside down and I didn't even realize it was happening.

"You didn't know because you've been too busy screwing around on her to pay attention!" Keri grabbed her keys and her purse. "Trisha, are you coming? I'm going home. This weekend is completely ruined."

Mac tried to reason with her, "Keri, just let her sort things out on her own for awhile. She obviously wants to be alone. Let's just try to have fun and salvage the rest of the weekend."

I felt like a piece of shit ruining this for everyone. "Just stay, I'm going to bed. I'll head home in the morning and see if I can talk to her."

Keri glared at me. "Why can't you just leave her alone and give her some space?"

"I want to apologize and make this right. I need to find her and make her understand."

"Understand what?" Trisha said. "Are you going to try and make her understand why you fooled around on her? Or maybe why you haven't even noticed that her life sucks? Maybe you'll try and explain how you could shove her to the ground and choke her. I think you should just leave her alone."

I decided I wasn't going to get anywhere tonight. I grabbed a beer and headed to my room. I tried to call Lindsey but she didn't answer. I knew she wouldn't want to talk to me. Hopefully she would make it home okay. I know I can make this up to her. I'll go home tomorrow and try and talk to her. I can't lose her. I won't lose her. She belongs to me.

Lindsey

That was the longest drive home. I could barely see through the tears as I tried to wrap my head around what had just happened. I know we've fought and argued a lot, but never, ever did he ever lay a hand on me before. My throat was sore and I couldn't tell if it was from the sobbing or from his hands on my neck. I looked in the mirror in the bathroom at the beach house as I was packing my things and I could see his handprints on my throat.

What was he thinking? My cell phone was lighting up with calls and texts from Michael, but they would all go unanswered. I had nothing to say to him, and there is nothing he could possibly say to make this better. Not now. It wasn't enough that he had admitted to screwing around on me, but to turn around and make it my fault was absolute bullshit.

Once I got home I was relieved to see that my mother wasn't home, not that I expected her to be. These days I was practically living at Keri's house anyway, and my mother wasn't around much. Between working and dating I never saw her anymore. We would talk every day, but I only saw her about once a week. I had gotten a text from her earlier that she would most likely be staying at her friend Andrea's house for the weekend because they were going to see a concert and do some shopping. She expected me to be gone anyway for the weekend.

It'll be nice to have the house to myself to think and try and figure out what's next. Maybe I would get a chance to see Rachel and talk to her. She lived a couple hours away but I guess I could drive up there tomorrow. I didn't love the thought of being alone for the weekend but with these marks on my throat it would be best if I stayed home and avoided a bunch of questions that I wouldn't know how to answer.

I pulled into the garage with my car and closed the door, another indicator to anyone driving by that I wasn't home. I wasn't in the mood for any visitors. My bag could wait until the morning. Right now all I wanted was a long, hot shower and my comfy bed.

I shed my clothes and hopped in the steamy shower. The hot water scalded my sunburned skin at first. I closed my eyes and tried to let the water wash away the nightmare of the evening I had just had. I wanted to be alone but at the same I needed to vent. I'd give anything at this moment for a relationship with my mom that would let me come to her with this. Or maybe if my sister was here. Rachel had her own life and her own problems. She didn't need to be bothered with mine.

After what felt like an hour in the shower, I toweled off and grabbed some comfy clothes ready to snuggle onto the couch for the night. Popcorn and some late night TV would be perfect right now. I went to the kitchen to start the popcorn and my phone lit up. Three text messages and two missed calls. Probably just Michael again. I checked and was surprised to see they were all from Rachel. Keri must've called her.

"Call me back and let me know you're okay."

"Text me when you get this so I know you made it home."

"If I don't hear back from you soon I'm calling Mom."

Well, I didn't want that. I picked up my phone and called her back. No answer. I texted her, "I'm home. Don't feel like talking about it. Call you to-morrow."

My phone buzzed right away with a new text. "Are you okay? What hap-pened?"

"I don't feel like talking about it."

"Come up here for a few days. It'll get your mind off things."

"We'll see. I just want to crash tonight. Call you in the A.M. Love you."

"Love you too."

Rachel was a great sister and going to see her for a few days would be good for me. If I let her see me like this though, what would she think of me? I'm not the kind of girl that lets her boyfriend push her around. Or am I? Michael has been messing around on me for who knows how long, and I just turned a blind eye to it. I felt absolutely pathetic.

The popcorn was done so I grabbed a bowl and hit the couch with my comfort food and my comfiest fleece blanket that Keri's mom bought me for my birthday. I flipped through the channels and of course nothing was on. I needed something to take my mind off today and Michael and the mess my life was currently in. I found a chick flick on TBS, *Serendipity*, which was always a go-to of mine. Why can't all men be as adorable and romantic as Jon Cusak? Maybe because I'm no Kate Beckingsale and my life is clearly not as great as this movie.

Dylan

I hadn't thought about Lindsey in awhile. At least, I tried not to think about her. Most of the time it worked and I just put her out of my mind. Although I have to admit I always asked Rachel about her sister. Hopefully she didn't notice that I was making it a point to ask. I tried to just casually add it into a conversation so she wouldn't wonder why I was asking. Truth is, it took months for me to shake that feeling I had after we kissed. I thought that there was something between us that night, but I must've misread her. She pushed me away the next day and told me she had no feelings for me and that the kiss was a mistake.

I knew she was still seeing that asshole Michael and that he was still screwing around on her. For a smart girl she was clueless. I never could understand what she saw in him.

"What a piece of shit!" she raged. Clearly Rachel was pissed after the call she got earlier. We were all at her and Troy's apartment having drinks when she got a call.

"Who was that on the phone? What's going on?" Troy asked. He, a couple of his friends from work, and I were all playing poker when Rachel came storming back into the room after taking the call.

"Keri, Lindsey's friend, called. Apparently a bunch of them rented a house in Galveston for the weekend and Lindsey and Michael got into a huge fight."

"What's new?" I sarcastically added. Realizing it was none of my business, and Rachel would get suspicious if I seemed too concerned, I decided I should shut up.

"Well, I know Dylan, but this time it went too far. Keri said he threw her on the ground and tried to choke her. Luckily a couple of the other guys pulled him off of her. I'm going to kill him when I get my hands on that piece of crap!"

I was horrified at the thought of that asshole putting his hands on her. It's bad enough that she's stayed with him while he ran around town screwing anything he could get his hands on, but now he's getting physically abusive?

All that time that had passed since that kiss hasn't changed anything about my feelings for her. I realize that it seemed impossible that there could ever be anything between us, but I still wish we could have given it a chance to see where things would've gone. Now she's older, I'm older, and things are different for us both. Of course, there's still Melissa. Melissa deserves better. I've never had the same feelings for her that she has for me. I do love her and we're good together. But that doesn't mean we should get married. She's been pressuring me to move in together and start planning a future. I'm just not ready for that. Not with her anyway.

"Hello? Where did you go?" Rachel was staring at me and I was completely oblivious.

I finally snapped out of it, "Sorry, I guess I got distracted for a minute."

"I can't believe he did this to her. And of course, when she needs her our mother is nowhere to be found. I've called her and she couldn't bother to answer. She just texted back that 'Linds will be fine. She's home just trying to figure things out.' She's not fine! She's scared and upset and she shouldn't be alone!" Rachel was fuming.

"Why don't you go home for a few days?" Troy chimed in finally. He knew better than to usually get involved in anything between Rachel and her family. Their situation wasn't good and Rachel was very defensive about things. She was beyond pissed at her mother and they had a rift between them for years that never seemed to go away. It only got worse as time went by.

"You know I'd do anything for my sister, but I'm not going home. I'll check on her in the morning. I'm going to text Keri and make sure she's coming back from the beach house tomorrow. I don't want her alone all weekend."

Rachel was right, Lindsey shouldn't be alone this weekend. Not only was she going to be upset about what happened, but there was a strong possibility that Michael would show up at her house. Who knew what kind of frame of mind he would be in when he did. If things were to escalate and no one was there he could really hurt her. If Rachel wasn't going, then I would.

50

I used to look at Linds as a little sister, someone to protect and watch over. But after the feeling between us the night we kissed, all of that changed for me. Regardless of whether she felt the same way I did, I felt like I needed to be there for her.

"I fold." I threw down my cards, facedown so no one would see that I had a pair of aces and a pair of jacks, a winning hand for sure. I knew if I was going to make the drive to Katy I'd have to leave soon. If I left now I could be there by eleven. Hopefully she would still be up.

"Geez Dylan, you were on such a hot streak! I guess your luck just ran out." Troy laughed as he lay down his hand with only a pair of eights queen high. "Grab me a beer too while you're up, D."

"Actually I'm heading out. I'm beat. I've done doubles all week and I've got three more next week. I'm just gonna head home and chill for the rest of the weekend."

No one would think any different. All summer I had been doing an internship at a local marketing firm and also working evenings tending bar at a local sports bar. I sometimes just liked to relax by myself by going for a run, a long bike ride, or a hike. Melissa was on a girls' trip to Vegas with some of the other girls from nursing school. They had all just passed their boards and would soon have their RN licenses. She wouldn't be back until Sunday. As long as I was reachable on my cell she wouldn't ask any questions. Besides, she seemed to be less dependent on me recently. She was always so clingy and possessive. Lately though, ever since she started her internship at Memorial, she was less needy and was starting to do things with her girlfriends and not always trying to spend every waking moment with me. I shouldn't complain because she really is an amazing woman. Smart, beautiful, and fun...the whole package.

For some reason though, I still couldn't shake that connection I felt that night with Lindsey. She asked me that night if I ever wished on stars. Until that night I never did, never even thought about it. I wasn't the "dreamer" type of guy. I believed in things that were real, tangible. I never noticed the stars or the moon and really took the time to think about them and their place in the universe. Now, I look up at the sky and I wonder if she sees what I see. Every now and then I wish on one of those stars just to see if it really works. I've wished for everything from my mom's health to passing my finals. Tonight I decided I would look up and wish that she was going to be okay. I just want her to be safe and happy.

Even if there wasn't anything between us, and if she has no feelings for me at all, I still want to see her. I want to know she's okay, mentally and physically. And I want to protect her from that asshole ever hurting her again.

I said goodbye to the guys and gave Rachel the usual hug on my way out the door. She was preoccupied texting and stressing about her sister. I knew how she felt. Rachel was like family to me, and if she was worried, upset, and angry, then so was I.

At my apartment I quickly packed an overnight bag with the essentials, grabbed a snack and a water for the road, and was back out the door in ten minutes flat. I stopped to gas up and grab a coffee to help keep me awake for the two-hour drive and a twelve pack that I iced down for once I got wherever I ended up later.

As I drove I wondered what the hell I was going to say to her when I showed up out of the blue on her doorstep. Would she throw me out? Last time I saw her she all but forced me to leave. Maybe things were different now. I wanted to be there for her to lean on. The night we talked on the steps at Chad's house felt so natural and easy. However this turns out, above all, we were like family connected by Rachel.

The next two hours seemed to take forever. The exits on I-10 felt like they were standing still. Only three more exits to go and then another ten minutes to the streets of that subdivision that I could drive with my eyes closed. I had no idea what would happen in the next two days while I was here. She may throw me out again and I would end up spending the weekend at Mom's watching baseball and eating too much pasta.

Finally I turned onto her street and suddenly I felt overwhelmed with fear. I must be completely out of my mind thinking this was a good idea. I haven't seen her in over a year and I'm just going to knock on the door and say, "Hey Linds, what's up?" I need to come up with something better than that, and quick. I've had two and a half hours to think about this and I've got nothing. I guess I should've wished on that star that this wouldn't completely blow up in my face.

Lindsey

I thought that a steamy shower, cup of hot tea, buttered popcorn, and a chick flick would help take my mind off things and maybe I'd be able to relax for awhile. I was mistaken.

Normally *Serendipity*, Jon Cusack, and popcorn is all I need on a Saturday night, but tonight is different. My head is spinning and my emotions are all over the place. I'm angry. I'm sad. I'm confused. Most of all I'm disappointed. Not with Michael so much as in myself. How could I continue to be in this relationship with someone who cheats on me, and now put his hands on me to hurt me physically. The mental and emotional hurt was bad enough, but this…this is just unforgivable. Oh, I'm sure he will come up with a million different excuses just like he does for everything else. Apparently he thought I was stupid and naïve enough to believe the lies over the past few months, but it wasn't hard to figure out that he was sleeping around behind my back. In case he hadn't noticed, there had been no sex between us since school let out for the summer. I couldn't bring myself to sleep with him knowing he'd been with someone else. I just kept myself busy enough and unattainable over the past few months hoping he wouldn't notice. How could he? He was still getting laid, just not by me.

It felt so good to have my own voice finally. I actually stood up for myself tonight. Maybe this was the beginning of me being me—Lindsey—not just me being Lindsey, Michael's girlfriend. With everything going on at home with my family maybe this was a good time for me to become more independent. Granted, I'm practically living with my best friend's family but they've made me feel like I'm one of them.

Maybe it's time for me to get off this couch and go have some fun instead of wallowing. I noticed cars at Chad's when I came home a few hours ago. I'm sure by now things are in full swing. What if Michael shows up though? Actually, who gives a shit?

I tried covering up the marks on my neck with a little makeup. They weren't too bad, but hopefully it was kind of dark inside the party so maybe no one would be able to tell. My hair was long and if I left it draped on my neck and shoulders you really couldn't see anything. It was about 90 degrees out still in the dead of the August heat, so normally my hair would be up off my shoulders, but I doubted anyone would think anything of it. I threw on a tank top and a short skirt, probably shorter than I normally would for fear of pissing off Michael, but tonight I didn't care. I had a body that would turn heads, but not in front of Michael. Guys just knew better. Michael made it clear that no one would look at, much less touch, his girlfriend. If anything was clear tonight it was me—that I'm not "his" anymore.

I decided to leave my car in the garage and walk to Chad's so that if anyone drove by they'd think no one was home. Michael will think maybe I went to Rachel's for the weekend. Chad's house is just a few blocks away and it's a beautiful night out so a walk would be perfect. I looked up to see lots of stars and a gorgeous full moon. Normally I would make a wish, but after today I just didn't know if I even believed in wishes anymore. I grabbed two beers from the fridge (Mom wouldn't notice if a couple were missing) and checked the mirror one more time. No one would be able to tell.

When I rounded the second block toward the party, I could see cars lined up and down the street. Must be the big end of the summer bash. Anyone who wasn't away at the beach would most likely be here. Most of these vehicles would still be here in the morning. We were all pretty conscious about not drinking and driving. The cops in the neighborhood were usually pretty cool about our parties unless fights broke out or the music got too loud.

As I got near the house I saw a bunch of the football players on the front steps of the house. Great…here come the questions.

"Lindsey? What the hell are you doing here?" Matthew Leonard, a senior and friend of Michael's stood up and looked at me like I had two heads. "Where's Michael? I thought you were all at the beach house for the weekend?"

"Wow…twenty questions?" I was not going to get into what happened with these guys. "I came home early. My mom needed me back for a family thing tomorrow so I came home a few hours ago. I wasn't tired and got bored sitting at home so I figured I'd walk down for a few minutes and see who's here."

They all just sat there looking at me as if they'd never seen me before. Actually they really hadn't seen me, just Lindsey, Michael's girlfriend.

"Why didn't he come back with you?" Now Jack Rios was chiming in on the grilling.

"He was drinking and had his truck so I just told him to stay and have fun with everyone else. Who's here?" I tried to divert the conversation away from Michael.

"The usual I guess." Jack was looking me up and down and not being very discreet about it.

"Well, I think I'll go in and see who's here and be social. Are you guys going to just sit out here all night by yourselves?"

Matt got up off the step and started to walk toward the door. "I'll go in with you, Linds."

"Matt, I don't need an escort, a babysitter, or a bodyguard." I turned and walked inside, conscious of the attitude and sarcasm in my tone.

I had a beer on the walk over and opened the second one once I was in the door. There were familiar faces everywhere, mostly people from our school, but some from neighboring schools as well. I made my way through the crowd past the keg and into the kitchen. Some of the other cheerleaders and football players were in there hanging out so I figured I better go in and be social. Now that I'm here though, I wish I was back on the couch in my jammies watching TV.

I stepped into the kitchen and was greeted with hugs and hellos from everyone and surprisingly no questions. My friend and fellow cheerleader Veronica leaned into whisper in my ear, "Keri called. We all know. But don't worry, no one is going to bring it up." She put her arms around me and gave me a tight hug. That was all I needed. Just a little break from what happened. I was thankful at that moment for my great friends, especially Keri. She knew me better than anyone else. I'm glad she anticipated that I would want to get out and wouldn't want twenty questions from everyone.

"Who wants a shot?" Chad was in rare form and clearly intending to enjoy his last weekend before school started the next week. "Linds! Let's do shots!"

"What the hell!" I had never been a big drinker but tonight I just didn't give a shit. It was time to come out of my shell and out of Michael's shadow and start living my life. "What are we drinking to?" I took my shot from Chad and raised it to cheers with him.

"Senior year, baby!!!" He was wasted and slurring his words already, and it was barely eleven.

We drank our shots and I immediately started feeling buzzed from the alcohol. I finished my second beer to wash down the shot and headed toward the keg to grab a cup and another beer.

For a little while I mingled through the crowd stopping to talk with friends along the way. I spotted Leslie, the one that Michael had been screwing around with, and once she saw me make eye contact with her she immediately left the party.

I made my way back into the kitchen where Chad and the majority of the other jocks had congregated. Flirting with any one of them would no doubt get back to Michael by the end of the night, and that was my goal in being here. But I knew none of them would betray Michael by paying any attention to me, so instead I went to where the guys from our rival school Cinco Ranch were by the keg.

It didn't take long for me to attract attention, especially with the outfit I was wearing tonight. I felt free tonight to be myself and not worry about someone constantly keeping track of what I was doing and who I was talking to.

I suddenly felt eyes burning a hole into me. I looked toward the kitchen and confirmed that I was being watched by Michael's teammates. I didn't care. Let them watch. Let them call him.

I filled my solo cup with the slightly cold draft beer that would no doubt make me feel like shit in the morning no matter how many I had, and went through the crowd to head back out onto the front porch. As much fun as I was having letting loose, I couldn't shake what had happened just a few hours ago. My whole world seemed to be turned upside down in a matter of six hours.

I suddenly felt like I couldn't breathe. All I could feel were his hands on my throat. I felt like the room was spinning. The combination of the alcohol and the emotional toll the evening had taken on me was too much. I needed air…now.

Once I was outside I took a few deep breaths and tried to steady myself again the side of the house. I had walked past the group of people congregating on the porch, down the steps, and around to the side of the house.

This was a bad idea. I'm not ready for this. I should've stayed home and gone to bed. I poured out my beer and turned around to leave.

"That's probably a good idea."

Startled, I turned around, my heart racing. That voice. I knew that voice. It was so dark I couldn't see anything. Just the shape of a man standing there a few feet from me. He started toward me. I panicked. He took another step toward me and as he did I could see his face lit by the almost full moon. Again, I exhaled. It was Dylan. It was always Dylan.

Dylan

I pulled in the driveway at her house and turned off the lights and ignition. No lights were on in the house. It looked empty. Damnit. What if she went back to the beach house? What if he hurts her again? What if something happened to her? I needed to get a handle on these questions that were swirling around in my head.

I walked around to the side of the house where I knew her bedroom was and there was total darkness in her room. No sign of her or anyone else for that matter. I knew it was wrong, but I grabbed the hidden key and went inside to make sure nothing had happened to her. The TV was on in the living room and the kitchen lights were on but no one was here. Rachel said she had come home, so where the hell was she?

There were keys on the kitchen counter. I picked them up and knew that they had to be hers. A single key to a Honda, two house keys, a small padlock key probably for her gym locker, a little cheer megaphone with an "L" on it, and a round silver keychain engraved on one side with 'Linds' and on the back, 'Love, Michael.'

"How cute," I said to myself sarcastically.

So her keys are here and she's not. I opened the door to the garage and there was her little red Honda Accord, a hand-me-down of course from Rachel. Poor Lindsey was always living in the shadow of her older sister. Rachel was the prodigy child. Straight-A student, salutatorian, sang in chorus, popular, and naturally beautiful Rachel had the full attention of everyone. While Lindsey, short and slightly awkward, average student, decent athlete, never quite got the attention she craved from her parents. It was like they spent it all on Rachel and had nothing left for her.

But Lindsey was beautiful. When she smiled at me on that porch last year she was stunning. Her eyes lit up and it felt as if she smiled at me with her entire body. She's petite, yet sexy. There's something about her that makes her seem more than just a young woman, as if she's already lived her life.

When I came around the block to her house I noticed the cars at Chad's. Maybe I should see if she's there. If she's not, then I'll have a few beers and then just head to Mom's house for the night.

It was almost a full moon and just a block and a half away so I figured I'd just leave my truck in the driveway and walk over. I had grabbed a twelve pack and iced it down in a cooler when I stopped for gas and a coffee before I left, so I grabbed two beers and started walking. As I came around the corner I could hear the music blaring. There would be a houseful of people celebrating the end of summer and the beginning of their senior year. Most likely I would know a few others that had already graduated and were either not yet off to college or had never left. Either way, there was only one person I cared about finding inside that house and that was Lindsey.

I walked up the driveway and past the many people standing around laughing and drinking. As I went up the steps I noticed a shadow on the side of the house. Slowly I descended the stairs and came around the corner of the house to see her leaning against the house. If the moon wasn't full I wouldn't have known it was her. She was alone. Walking toward her she didn't notice me at first. I watched her pour out what I can only assume was beer from her cup and turn to leave. I didn't mean to startle her.

"That's probably a good idea," I whispered, trying not to scare her. She froze and stared for a moment.

"Dylan? What are you doing here?"

I couldn't tell from her tone or response whether she was surprised or scared. Not wanting to scare her I slowly stepped forward into the light from the moon so she could see that it in fact was me.

"Sorry Linds, I didn't mean to scare you."

Defensively she answered, "You didn't scare me. I was just getting ready to leave."

"I was looking for you." I wanted her to know that I wasn't just here because I had nothing better to do.

"Why were you looking for me? Don't you have better things to do with your time?"

Lindsey was being sarcastic as usual. Considering what she had been through earlier today I'm not surprised at her mood. I knew I would have to tread lightly. She would be defensive, understandably so, and would probably not feel much like talking. But regardless, I wanted to be there for her in any way that I could.

"Do you want me to walk you back to your house and we can talk?" I was treading lightly. I didn't want to spook her. "Or I can just walk with you and make sure you get home okay."

Her eyes filled with tears but she wouldn't let them fall. "I don't need a babysitter, Dylan. And I don't need a therapist either."

"What do you need then?" All I wanted was to hold her and make it all go away. I could tell that she wanted to break down, let the tears flow, and simply fall apart. But in typical Lindsey style, she dug her heels in instead.

"Nothing from you. I don't NEED anything or anyone. I just want to be alone."

She walked past me brushing lightly against my bare skin with hers. Before she could get past me I turned instinctively and grabbed her by the arm. My grip was light, not aggressive at all, but still she reacted.

"Let go of me!" she yelled.

Everyone that was on the porch steps froze and stared at us. I could tell she wanted to become invisible at that very moment. Her lip began to quiver and the tears again welled up in her eyes. This time she couldn't hold them back. They poured from her eyes like the dam had just broken. She looked like she was going to faint. Just as she started, I scooped her up in my arms and started walking. She went limp in my arms and buried her face in my neck. She cried quietly as I carried her the two blocks to her house.

As we got closer to the house she fell quiet. I wasn't sure if she was drunk and had passed out, or what exactly was going on with her.

"Why are you here, Dylan?" she whispered into my neck. I could feel hear breath on my skin and it sent a fire through me like I had never felt before.

I said nothing. I just stopped walking and couldn't speak. Why was I here? This had nothing to do with me whatsoever. She's not my girlfriend. She's not even really my friend. What the fuck was I doing trying to play knight-in-shining-armor to someone who made it clear once before that she felt nothing for me?

She lifted her head and our eyes were inches apart. Our lips were so close I could almost taste her lip gloss. I wanted to kiss her. In spite of how rejected I felt after what happened before, I still wanted her. I needed to tell her why I was here.

"I'm here for you, Linds. I came here to make sure you were okay. I needed to know you were safe and that he wouldn't hurt you again."

Lindsey

What was he doing here and why am I in his arms? I don't care about any of that right now, honestly. I feel safe, and that's all I need right now. I'm not sure what just happened back there at the party, but I felt like I couldn't breathe. My head was spinning and I thought I was going to pass out. I feel so childish that he thinks he needs to rescue me.

"Why are you here, Dylan?" I asked.

It seemed like it took forever for him to answer. I lifted my head from where it was buried in his neck, the smell of his cologne was all over my face. It was intoxicating. He was intoxicating. I looked into his eyes and just froze.

He just stared at me with those eyes, those beautiful cobalt blue eyes. "I'm here for you Linds. I came here to make sure you were okay. I needed to know you were safe and that he wouldn't hurt you again."

I didn't know what to say. How did he even know? Rachel. Of course it was Rachel.

I started to let go of him, "Can you put me down? I don't need your help. I'm not some stray dog that needs rescuing."

We had reached the front porch of my house and he gently lowered me onto the bench under the covered area. He sat down in one of the chairs and fell silent.

I was being bitchy but I couldn't help myself. I wanted to put up a wall. The last thing I needed was another man thinking that he needed to take care of me. Besides, Dylan always treated me like a kid. All I was to him was Rachel's little sister, and that's all I'd ever be.

Maybe that kiss had changed things for him and how he saw me now? Unfortunately, I never gave him the opportunity to find out. I was so worried about Michael that I had pushed Dylan away. If I had known then how things would turn out, I might not have asked him to leave.

After a long awkward pause, he broke the silence, "Do you want to talk about it?"

"Talk about what?" Lord only knows what Rachel had made this out to be. And besides, I'm pissed now that she told him. Why would she think it's something he should know about?

"Linds, I was at Rachel and Troy's when Keri called and told her what happened with you and Michael. She's really concerned about you. She wanted to come home and be here for you, but she said you told her you wanted to be alone."

"I did want to be alone. I do. So why would you think you needed to come here, Dylan?"

"I don't know what came over me. I just packed a bag and left. I wanted to see that you were okay."

He couldn't look at me. His eyes were staring up at the sky. The moon was full and it lit up his face so bright as he tilted his head back against the chair and gazed at it. God, he was beautiful. That chiseled profile of his sent a charge through my body when I looked at him.

"Thank you," I whispered as I looked away, the tears again welling up in my eyes. Just a few hours ago I was on my back being choked by a guy I thought loved me. And now here I sat with bruises from him on my neck. Across from me, was a man who on a whim dropped everything to drive over two hours just to make sure I was not alone. This man who I used to fantasize about being with, who I thought would never know me as more than just his friend's little sister, is real and is sitting right here wanting to take care of me. It was almost too much to process. I was so tired, emotionally and physically, all I wanted to do was lay down and close my eyes.

He was silent. I knew when he kissed me and I turned him away I had hurt him. I guess at the time I figured it was just a bruised male ego. But was there more to it? Was it really possible that he felt something for me other than just friendship?

I stood up and turned to him with my arm outstretched to his. He stood and turned as if to walk toward his truck to leave.

"Please don't go. Stay with me."

He froze, clearly taken back by my sudden change of heart. But he kept walking to his truck, my heart sinking. He didn't even turn to say goodbye. What did I expect though? I had rejected him before and tonight I hadn't been any more welcoming or affectionate.

I couldn't believe he was leaving. There was no way I could stand here and just watch him drive away. Defeated, I turned to walk into the house, I heard the truck door shut and waited to hear the engine start. But nothing. Then I felt his hand gently on my shoulder. I turned to see him standing there with a bag and a cooler.

"Did you really think I would leave you?" He smirked at me and grabbed my hand. "Come on, let's go inside and let me be here for you."

Dylan

There was no way in hell I was leaving her. Even if she put up a fight and told me to go I would've camped out in the driveway in my truck before I'd leave her here alone this weekend. If that asshole came here to talk to her he would have to deal with me first. He would never lay another hand on her, and I would make sure of it.

Lindsey and I both separately changed into some comfy clothes and while she was in the bathroom I opened a beer for myself and made her a cup of tea. I had seen the half drank cup she must've had before she went to the party, so I made her a fresh one. She needed to be cared for and nurtured. Whatever she needed, I was going to be there for her.

This seems so crazy that I'm here. I've got a life in Austin with Melissa, and that life is actually pretty good. Pretty good should be enough, right? I just haven't been able to shake that feeling I had when Lindsey and I kissed last year. When she rejected me and I went back to school, I just went on with things as they were before. But in the back of my mind, and my heart, she was always there.

"You made me tea?" She seemed surprised and pleased. I could imagine Michael probably never treated her the way she should be treated.

"Do you want something different? I can get you a beer or water or…"

"Stop. The tea is fine. It's perfect actually. No one has ever done that for me." She took the mug from my hand and set it down on the counter. She took both of my hands in hers and leaned into my chest. "Thank you," she whispered into my chest.

"You don't have to thank me. There's nowhere else I'd rather be than here with you right now."

"Nowhere?" Lindsey looked at me with those eyes. Those beautiful hazel eyes were piercing through me. She smirked at me and I could feel my whole body heat up like a sauna. "What about the couch? Wouldn't you like to be there with me right now?"

If she was trying to torture me, it was working. Just thinking about being with her was making me hard. Thoughts were racing through my mind about kissing those lips, touching her body, and feeling her skin against mine.

"Linds, I think the last thing you need right now is to make things more complicated than they already are." As much as I wanted her, I cared more about her needs than my own and I didn't want to add anything else to the situation to make things worse. "We're not going to do anything that you're uncomfortable with."

"Dylan, I've wanted this for a long time."

She moved to sit on the couch, so I sat down next to her. I touched the side of her face with my right hand and gently slid the other behind the back of her head and slowly pulled her into me. Our bodies pressed together and I hoped that she couldn't feel how aroused I was already. My lips touched hers and carefully I kissed her slowly and lightly. I felt her lean into me and I knew she was feeling the same thing I was at that moment. The gentleness of our kissing became more intense as our lips parted and we let our tongues take over. She moved onto my lap facing me, her legs straddled around me. Her hands moved up my back and mine explored her body cautiously. Our breathing was increasingly heavy and we were moving our bodies against each other as our kissing intensified.

I broke from her lips and moved to her neck, kissing gently with my lips and grazing my tongue along her shoulder. She moaned and pressed her hips into mine. I could tell she felt my hardness because she continued pressing against me making me more aroused by the minute.

I wanted this so much, but at what cost? What about Melissa? Things weren't perfect with her, but she loves me, and she's put up with more than her share of crap from me. She didn't deserve this. And this will only make a bad situation worse for Lindsey. We are in two totally different places in our lives and she's way too young to get into something this complicated with me, Michael, and Melissa.

"What's wrong?" I didn't realize she was now staring at me as I had broken from our kissing. "You're somewhere else. Dylan, what is it?"

She looked hurt and confused. I moved her gently off my lap and next to me draping her legs across mine.

"I just don't know if this is right. You've been through something traumatic today and you're hurt and reeling from what happened with Michael. And I'm not the guy that cheats on his girlfriend. It's just not who I am. As right as this feels, it's wrong."

"Dylan, I want this. I want you. I've fantasized about this moment for years."

I saw confusion and hurt in her eyes. It would be so easy for me to just ignore my conscience and take her in my arms and not look back.

"Linds, I'm sorry. You have to know how badly I want this, how bad I want you. But you know it's not right. It's not the right time for us. We need to sort through our stuff first. Where would we even go from here if we started something this way?"

"I know, you're right, but will you at least stay with me tonight?" She lifted her head and gently kissed my cheek. "Dylan, thank you. Thank you for being the good guy. And thank you for coming here tonight."

"There's nowhere else I would be. If you need me, I will always be here for you."

She looked up at me with those sparkling eyes and smiled. I knew in that moment this was just the beginning of our story. We spent the next hour just lying there on the couch talking and kissing, her wrapped up in my arms.

Lindsey

The next morning, I woke up on the couch wrapped in a blanket and looked over to see Dylan asleep in the recliner. The past twenty-four hours had been an absolute whirlwind. My head was throbbing, partially from the alcohol, and probably the rest from the crying.

I went to the kitchen and grabbed two Advil and a Dr. Pepper, then started a small pot of coffee for Dylan. I knew from years of watching him with Rachel that he was a morning coffee drinker, cream no sugar.

My phone was on the charger in the kitchen and undoubtably had numerous texts and missed calls. I thought about checking it before I got in the shower, but I selfishly wanted just a few minutes of peace.

I left Dylan sleeping while I took a long shower trying to wrap my head around everything that happened yesterday. I knew I would have to face Michael at some point. Even though I walked out on him last night and ended our relationship, he's not going away. Michael doesn't give up that easily. He's not going to just let me go without a fight. We've had our share of arguments but last night was different. I saw something change in him and it scared me. I knew it was over with him when I confirmed that he had been sleeping around, but putting his hands on me…there's no coming back from something like that.

I felt sad that after several years of sharing all my high school memories up until now with him that it's just over. I loved him, and a part of me always would. Our senior year was supposed to be full of great memories together, but that was all over now. All of our friends are intermingled and things would never be the same again for us. My best friend is dating his best friend. It will be awkward, but I can't live like this anymore.

And then there was that guy sleeping in the recliner. I still can't believe he came here, for me. Rachel must've told him what happened after Keri undoubtedly called her last night. But why would Dylan feel he needed to drive two hours to come here for me? I know I hurt him that day last year when I told him to leave after he kissed me. But honestly, I didn't think he would dwell on it, or on me for that matter. He's got a life and a girlfriend back at school. So what in the world does he want with me?

I closed my eyes and breathed in the steam from the shower trying to figure out what was next. Why can't I just get away from it for a day or two and just breathe for a few minutes?

A knock on the door startled me and my eyes quickly opened.

"Linds? You okay?" Dylan sounded hoarse and groggy.

I peeked my head around the shower curtain and smiled. "Good morning. Did you get any sleep?"

"Are you kidding me? The way you snore?" He smirked at me flashing those adorable dimples. His hair was slightly messy and he had a dark stubble on his chiseled face that made him look sexier than normal.

"I do not snore!" I yelled as I splashed water at his face. He came inside the bathroom and over to the shower where I stood naked behind the curtain. My neck was bruised from Michael's hands and I didn't want him to see me like that.

I pulled the curtain closed. "I'll be out in a minute." Suddenly I was terrified that he would open the curtain and see me for who I was. The eighteen year old short, underdeveloped little sister of his best friend. No man would possibly find that attractive.

"Want help in there?"

I peeked my head out again, "Ummm, weren't you the one who turned me down last night? Had a change of heart have you?"

"Well, a guy can change his mind right?"

"Dylan, you were right last night. We need to think this through before we do something that we can't take back."

He leaned in and kissed me, gently on that one little freckle on my nose. His hands reached up and held my face and I started to cry. I just wanted this to all go away and for things to be uncomplicated. He reached in and turned off the shower, grabbed a towel and wrapped it around me.

"It's going to be okay, Linds."

We both sat on the bathroom floor and he held me while I cried. I cried for the end of my relationship with Michael. I cried for my family and the inevitable changes that were about to take place and would no doubt change my life forever. I cried because I knew that I already loved this man who I may never be able to have.

Melissa

 ylan wasn't answering his phone, but honestly I was almost relieved that he didn't pick up. I hated lying to him, so by not having to talk to him then technically I wouldn't have to lie.

I had told him I was off on a girl's trip to celebrate passing our nursing boards. That wasn't exactly the whole truth. I was celebrating passing my boards, but I was also indulging in a weekend away at a spa resort in Southern California Wine Country. And the second part of that lie was that I wasn't on a girls' trip. I was the only girl here this weekend. But I wasn't alone.

Kyle was here too. In fact, the last three times I was away on a "girl's weekend" I was actually with him. I knew it was wrong, and I knew that either it had to end with Kyle or I had to leave Dylan. I couldn't continue to have it both ways. The stress of lying was getting to me and I hated myself for doing this to Dylan.

In my defense, Dylan had been dragging his feet with this relationship and always putting me second to everything else in his life. Things had been a little better this past year or so, but still we weren't living together or even talking about making any steps to move forward with our relationship. I wanted to get married and have a family, and I didn't want to wait forever. Who knew if Dylan would ever be ready for that?

I met Kyle at the hospital when I was doing my internship in the Developmental Treatment Department at St. Joseph's Cancer and Research Center. He was a second year resident working in the lab assisting the chief of oncology with an experimental stem cell clinical trial.

Kyle was grounded and stable. He was three years older than me and knew what he wanted out of life. And he was definitely not afraid to go after what he wanted.

One night after a long shift, the other interns and I decided to stop for drinks since the next day was a Saturday and no one had to get up early for once. We took cabs about ten blocks uptown to a sports bar near the more upscale suburban area of Austin, instead of our usual hangouts near campus.

We piled into a corner booth with a couple pitchers of beer and ordered some wings and other appetizers. After a couple beers I headed to the ladies' room. As I rounded the corner down the short hallway to the restroom, I bumped right into someone coming around the corner. It was Kyle.

"Oh my gosh, I'm so sorry," I was horrified that I had just spilled his drink down the front of his white shirt.

He didn't seemed rattled at all. "It's okay, really. I didn't like this shirt anyway." He smiled at me and I felt a charge through my body. "I'll let you buy me another drink to make up for it."

Was he was flirting with me?

"Um, yeah, sure!" I was caught off guard by this. "Just let me use the restroom and I'll be right back."

I turned toward the ladies' room and then quickly turned back around before he had a chance to run away. "Why don't you just join us?"

Oh my god, what was I doing? I'm assuming he was flirting with me, and what if he wasn't. What if he's here with someone? He must be with a girlfriend, or at the very least a date or something. I mean, look at him. Thick, wavy blonde hair and huge blue eyes…no way is he single.

"I'd love to. Let me just ditch my date and I'll be right over."

I must've looked horrified because he immediately started laughing.

"I'm kidding!" he said with a laugh as he turned to walk away.

He left me standing there not knowing what the hell just happened. I went into the restroom and took one look at my face. What a disaster! I looked like I was sunburned my face was so flushed. Get your shit together, Melissa.

I used the restroom, splashed a little cold water on my face, washed my hands, and headed toward the table. I just about froze when I saw him sitting at the end of our booth with a chair pulled up. I didn't think he'd actually want to join us.

"Hey," I said awkwardly as I returned to the table, "you all know Kyle, right?"

Everyone just looked at me like I had two heads.

"I ran into him, literally, in the hall and invited him to join us."

Kyle just smirked at me. He could obviously tell I was slightly uncomfortable for some reason. I tried to shake it off, but my poker face wasn't that great.

We all had a few more beers and slowly one by one the others started leaving. And then there were two. Just me and Kyle. Crap, this was not good.

"So, looks like it's just you and me."

Suddenly I felt uncomfortable. He wasn't making me uncomfortable in a bad way, more like in a he's-so-gorgeous-and–charming-and-I-need-to-leave-now-or-I-won't-want-to-leave kind of way.

"I really should get going too." I stood and reached for my coat in the booth.

Kyle stood quickly and helped me with my coat. Well, that's never happened to me before.

"Can I help you get a cab or give you a ride somewhere?" He was sweet to offer but what would I tell Dylan? Oh, who was I kidding? Dylan wouldn't even ask how or when I got home. All he knew was I was going out for drinks after work with some friends and I'd see him tomorrow afternoon sometime.

"Sure, that would be great. Actually I don't live too far from here and it's nice out. We could walk for a bit if you want to." Suddenly I was not nervous anymore at the thought of being alone with him.

He turned to me and held out his arm, "I'd love to escort you home."

We left the bar around 12:30, and after a ten-block walk that took about a half hour but seemed like it went way too fast, we were in front of the duplex where I shared a half house with my roommate, Shelly.

"Well, this is me." Then it dawned on me that I had no idea where he lived. He could be completely across town from his place and his vehicle was still at the sports bar. "I'm so sorry, I never even thought that this might not be on your way. And what about your vehicle?"

"I shouldn't be driving anyway. I'll just see if I can catch a cab." He reached in his pocket for his cell phone to call.

"Wait," I stopped him and touched his arm. "Why don't you come inside and we can have another drink or a cup of coffee or something while you call and wait?"

He put his phone back in his pocket, reached for my hand, "I'd really like that."

That night in my apartment, he never called a cab. Instead we sat on the couch talking and drinking coffee until about 4 A.M. He was so easy to talk to and was such a complete gentleman. He knew I had a boyfriend and didn't make any gesture whatsoever to be inappropriate and make a move on me. Although he did tell me several times that if I didn't have a boyfriend he wouldn't have been such a gentleman. Clearly we were attracted to each other, but I didn't feel right about acting on it.

Eventually that night, we fell asleep on opposite ends of the couch, as friends. At some point, he must've woken up, covered me with a blanket, and left. He wrote a note on a napkin before he left. It said, "Liss, what an unexpected but wonderful night, K."

"Oh shit," I thought, "I'm in trouble."

That was almost ten months ago, and ever since that night Kyle and I had been developing a relationship. At first, it was a flirty friendship with lots of lunches, coffee dates, and late night talks on the couch with wine.

One of those late night talks took our friendship to a different level. I knew it was probably inevitable, but I also knew that I wasn't going to be the one to initiate the first kiss.

I was telling him about my relationship with Dylan and how I was tired of waiting for him to be ready to take the next step to move forward with me.

He leaned toward me and touched the side of my face, his touch sending a chill through my body. I was so attracted to him, but I truly loved Dylan.

"You deserve more, Liss. He's never going to grow up and fully commit to you." He leaned in and pressed his lips to mine, gently at first, until my lips parted and welcomed his tongue. The surge that went through me was so intense, like nothing I had felt before. The months of anticipation leading up to this moment only made it more surreal.

There was nothing in me that wanted to tell him to stop, so I didn't.

We spent what felt like an hour on the couch kissing, touching and exploring each other, just getting to know what the other responded to. The yoga pants and tank top I was wearing didn't leave much to the imagination and provided ample opportunity for his hands to discover my body. I could feel his arousal when we pressed our bodies together. His hand went around my back and started to slide down the back of my pants, and again, I didn't stop him.

His hands made their way down to feel just how wet I had gotten from his kiss and his touch. He gently circled around my clit making me moan and grind against him harder. I could definitely feel his hardness through his jeans when I pressed myself against him and I reached down to stroke him. As I let my hand feel the outline of him, he gently slid a finger inside me and I thought I would come undone.

He pulled his lips from mine slightly and whispered, "Are you sure this is what you want?"

"I've never been more sure of anything," I said as I reached for his hand and stood up from the couch. I knew this was wrong, but it felt amazing. He was an incredible man who knew what he wanted in life, and right now he wanted me.

We reached my bedroom and I lit a few candles on the nightstand next to the bed. If this was going to happen, we might as well make it the most it could be. He brought the wine bottle and glasses with him and poured us both a little more to drink. I looked around at this romantic setting. I'd never experienced anything like this before with Dylan, or anyone for that matter. Dylan's idea of romance was making it into the bedroom and dimming the light in the bathroom for ambiance.

We drank a little more of our wine, kissing and touching all the while. The anticipation was building and we were both ready for this moment.

I lifted his shirt over his head and kissed his chest lightly. He had an amazing body and I let my fingertips move across his chest, stomach, and down to the top of his jeans. I unbuttoned the top and slid the zipper down. His hands grabbed the side of my face and he kissed me deeply while I started to slide his jeans down his thighs. He sat down on the edge of the bed and let his jeans come all the way off. I stood in between his legs while he lifted my tank top, kissing and touching my breasts. His hands slid down my back, catching the waist of my pants and sliding them down as he went. I had nothing on underneath so I stood there completely undressed and unguarded, but I was surprisingly comfortable.

He pulled me onto him gently and slowly. I gasped and threw my head back as he went deep inside me, his lips on my breasts and his hands on the small of my back. I moved with the rhythm of his hips and let him take the lead and he thrust himself inside me again and again. I could tell he was holding back, waiting for me to climax before he finished. He was holding me tightly and pressing me into him, whispering in my ear "I want you to cum, Liss," and as he did, I let go and completely lost myself. Seconds later I could feel him reaching orgasm with me as I continued to come undone.

I thought I would be nervous my first time with him, yet I felt more at ease than I expected. We made love twice that night and once again in the morning when we woke.

That night was the start of something that I just couldn't walk away from no matter how hard I tried. Since that night we had gone on a few weekend getaways when I could find time. I hated lying to Dylan and at this point I was just trying to find the right time to end things with him. I knew that Dylan would never be ready to commit the way I wanted. I loved Dylan but I was falling in love with Kyle.

Two calls to Dylan last night went unanswered as well as another this morning. He said he was going to Rachel and Todd's to play poker last night, so maybe he stayed and is sleeping off a hangover. I'd try him again later, but now...Kyle.

Michael

$\mathcal{I}$ spent the rest of the night alone in my room that I should've been sharing with Lindsey. How did things go so wrong so quickly last night? She had forgiven me for a lot over the years, but this may be too much for her to get over. It's bad enough that I cheated on her, but to have put my hands on her was more than crossing the line.

Three voicemails and eight text messages to her had all gone unanswered. Last night I wanted to go after her, but the guys were right to make me stay here. I'd had a few beers, so driving was out of the question.

Leslie meant nothing to me, so breaking that off with her wouldn't phase me. How pathetic to let a meaningless fling ruin three years with Lindsey.

I hit redial again, hoping that maybe this time she would answer. Voicemail again. "Linds, it's me again. I don't know what to say other than I'm so so sorry about everything. Please just let me make this up to you. Call me back. Please Lindsey. I love you. I can't live without you."

She wasn't going to answer, so I had no choice but to go see her. I headed downstairs to see if anyone else was up and around.

Trisha and Keri were at the counter having coffee when I walked into the kitchen. I could cut the tension with a knife and it was obvious what they were talking about since the conversation abruptly ended the second I walked into the room.

"Hey, are the guys still asleep?" I asked, trying to break the ice with the girls. It would've been easier if Chris and Mac were up, but they would no doubt sleep until noon. I tossed and turned most of the night trying to figure out how to fix this mess I'd made of things.

"What the hell got into you last night, Michael?" Keri was glaring at me and I wished at this moment that I had gone after Lindsey last night. If the guys would've let me I'd be with her now trying to make things right with her.

"I don't know. I just lost it. It'll never happen again, I promise."

Keri stood and walked toward me. She stopped just inches from me and glared at me with contempt. She drew her hand back and with amazing force she slapped me across my left side cheek with her open palm.

"I will never let you hurt her again." She stood there shaking and tears gently fell from her eyes. "She's like a sister to me, and I will not stand by and watch you do this to her. She's had enough sadness and disappointment in her life lately. The fact that you're so out of touch with what's happening with her makes me sick. She deserves better than you."

She was right, Lindsey deserved better than this…better than me. I was going to prove to her how sorry I was and that I can chance and be the man she deserved to be with.

"What can I do? I'll do anything to make this up to her and to both of you. I love her and I don't want to lose her." I knew if I wanted any chance to get Lindsey back I'd have to win over her friends.

Trisha got up to leave the room. She turned and said, "How about not physically and emotionally hurting her anymore. That would be a great place to start. I don't know if she will forgive you for this. She's taken a lot from you this past year. She's known about Leslie for awhile now."

I had no idea she knew. Why hadn't she said anything to me? It made sense now why she hadn't wanted to be intimate with me lately. I guess I figured she was just wanting a break.

"She should've said something to me."

Trisha looked disgusted and started to laugh. "So, let me get this straight, you would've stopped seeing Leslie if Lindsey said something to you? That's the most ridiculous crap I've ever heard."

"That's not what I meant, Trisha. I just wish I had known. Maybe I would've ended it awhile ago, I don't know." And that was the truth, I didn't know what I would've done. All I knew now was that I had to make this right with her now. I would do whatever I had to do to win her back and make her trust me again. I wasn't going to lose her. I couldn't live without her.

I packed up my stuff and started getting ready to leave. Some of her things were still here too, so I grabbed them and tossed them into my bag. I'd go straight to her house from here and beg her to forgive me.

The girls said to give her space, but I needed to see her and explain. I didn't know how to apologize for any of what happened yesterday, but I was going to try anything I could.

I loaded my things into the truck and took off. It was a long drive home so I'd have plenty of time to think of what to say to her. Hopefully she would be there. If not, I'd just wait. That's all I could do.

All I could do was just hold her while she cried. I knew that's what she needed from me, and I'd do anything to make her stop hurting.

We sat there on the bathroom floor for awhile before she finally stopped shaking. When she looked up at me, her hazel eyes had turned an even more beautiful deep bright emerald. I leaned in and gently kissed that adorable single freckle on the end of her nose.

She smiled at me with her eyes, then leaned in and kissed me. The energy between us was undeniable. I fought it last night, but today in the light of the day I didn't want to resist it anymore.

I broke away from the kiss.

"I want this, Linds. More than you know."

She smiled and lightly bit her lip, "Dylan, I've wanted this for a long, long time."

I stood and helped her up, holding her hands in mine, her body still slightly damp and wrapped in a towel. I led her into her bedroom where we had shared a kiss last year.

We stood at the edge of the bed. My shirt was wet from holding her head against my chest. I started to pull it off and she stopped me.

She took hold of it and slid it up over my head with no resistance from me. Her hands traced down the front of my chest, to my stomach, and the top of my jeans. When her hands reached the top button, she looked up at me and smiled with her eyes.

Slowly, she unbuttoned the top button and lowered the zipper. I pushed my jeans down and tugged them off at the ankles.

She ushered me down to a seated position on the edge of the bed and stood in front of me. I pulled her in between my legs and reached for the towel that was tied around her breasts. I hesitated, waiting to see if she was apprehensive. Her hands reached up to mine and I thought she was going to stop me, but she helped my fingers untuck the towel. It fell to the ground leaving her completely exposed and vulnerable to me.

I softly kissed her stomach and could feel her shiver as her breathing increased. Her hands ran through my hair and I let mine explore her backside. My lips moved from her stomach up to her breasts. I slowly kissed around her cleavage, eventually letting my tongue move to her nipples. As my movement became more aggressive I could hear her starting to moan as she threw her head back with pleasure. I moved my hands down her legs and up in between them to feel her arousal. I teased her with my fingertips and she moved with the motion as I massaged her slowly at first then faster until I could feel that she was getting close to climaxing.

I stopped and pulled her onto my lap so she could feel how aroused she was making me. She straddled me and I pulled her into me, moving our hips together as we passionately kissed with our tongues, our hands all over each other's bodies.

I broke from the kiss momentarily, "You're sure this is what you want?"

She didn't answer me.

She smiled, resumed our kiss, and I had my answer.

I didn't know what to expect. I could only assume that Michael was the only man she'd been with before now. I was careful to let her initiate each step and lead the way.

She moved onto her back and I moved in next to her, touching her softly with my fingers and lips. I was hesitating nervously, worried that this was too much for her after what she had just been through yesterday.

She must've sensed that I was holding back.

"Dylan, I'm sure. I promise you, this is what I want. I need this."

Lindsey

I woke up in his arms, still shaking slightly from what had just happened between us. I knew it was real, he was here and we just made love. Yet I still couldn't believe it was true.

Dylan was sleeping, so I just lay there watching him. His five o'clock shadow had now turned into a short stubbly beard that had done a number on my face for the last hour or so. But I wasn't complaining by any means.

Our legs were intertwined, his arm underneath my head and I could hear his heart beating as my face lay on his chest. He was attentive and careful and gentle with me, something I hadn't experienced before with Michael.

Michael. He would no doubt keep calling, texting, and trying to get me to talk to him until he succeeded. Too bad he didn't put that much effort into being a good, faithful boyfriend and none of this would've happened.

I left my phone on the charger in the kitchen all night and avoided it earlier. At some point, I would have to answer the calls and texts and speak to Michael about what happened. He would be desperate to fix things like he always did each time he screwed up.

In the past I always forgave him for everything. Too many times to count he would cause a horrible argument and then days, sometimes even just hours, later he would bring me flowers and apologize.

I was weak, insecure, and I always let him convince me that 'it would never happen again.' But it always did, and it recently had started to happen more often, so that it felt like we were fighting more than not.

Michael would make me feel like it was my fault for arguing with him, and for pushing him too far. So often he manipulated me into believing that I was the problem, and that if I was a better girlfriend we wouldn't fight. I had no self-esteem and no backbone when it came to him.

Recently I had confided in Keri's parents about my college dilemma regarding finances. They knew all about what had been happening at home with my family, and they'd practically adopted me into their family.

Keri's mom asked me once if Michael had been abusing me, physically or emotionally. It came as such a surprise to me when she broached the subject. She told me about the abuse that she had endured with the man she had been married to briefly prior to Keri's dad.

She must have seen the signs. I had become less social with my friends and I was always nervous and trying to please everyone. I apologized even when I had done nothing wrong.

At the time I didn't understand what she meant, but now it all became alarmingly clear that Michael in fact had not only been physically abusive last night, but he had been emotionally controlling me for years.

I knew that it was time for me to make a break from him and start putting my life together for myself. My decision had been made that I would stay with the Williams', work, and after graduation start classes at University of Houston.

It would be a long senior year dealing with the fallout of our breakup, not to mention the looming inevitable demise of my mother's marriage that would ultimately change things for me.

And now there was this. Dylan, and whatever this was happening between the two of us. I knew I didn't regret being with him, but I wasn't naïve enough to think that this wasn't going to be extremely complicated.

There was Michael obviously. And Dylan's girlfriend, Melissa. They had been dating a long time, and there would be an ugly fallout from this I'm sure.

But Rachel was going to be the biggest hurdle to get past if anything was going to come of this new development with Dylan and me. She and Dylan had been best friends since grade school so there was no way she would be okay with the two of us together.

I was starting to get ahead of myself and letting my mind wander. Dylan was still asleep, so I decided to try and sneak out of bed without waking him. As I slid out from underneath his arm and the covers, he stirred but never woke up. I put on a pair of sweats and grabbed his t-shirt and threw it on over my head. The intoxicating smell of him all over me was sending chills through me and I stopped for a moment, lifted the shirt up to my face and took in his scent. I looked back at him lying in my bed and thought to myself, *This is really happening.*

In the kitchen I decided to face the music and turn my phone on finally. As I waited for it to power up, my stomach twirled in circles and I suddenly felt nauseous. I knew that the messages that would no doubt be waiting would be from Michael and Rachel, both of whom I wasn't ready to speak with yet.

The notifications started dinging as soon as the phone came to life. A total of three voicemails and twelve text messages were waiting for me. I opened the voicemail first, and there were two from Michael, and one from Rachel.

I listened to Rachel's first. "Call me when you get this. It's around 9 A.M. And I'm thinking of coming home for a few days to help you deal with this mess going on. Talk to you soon. Love you."

I would need to call her quickly and make sure she wasn't already on her way. She would not be happy to walk in on Dylan in my bed and me in his shirt.

The phone rang three times and then went to voicemail. I hung up and texted her, "Hey, got your voicemail. Sorry I was sleeping in. Don't come home, I'm fine. Just gonna chill today. I'll try calling you again in a bit. Love you."

The voicemails from Michael were all over one minute long each. I didn't even listen to them, but I didn't delete them either.

The twelve texts were a mixture of Rachel, Michael, Keri, and Trisha. The girls were all just checking to see if I was doing okay. And Michael's were all full of "I'm sorry" and "It'll never happen again" and "What can I do to fix this?"

Well, Michael I don't think this is fixable. I didn't bother to message him back, but I did send a group text to Keri and Trisha letting them know I was okay and just staying home for the day.

I set my phone down and grabbed two mugs for coffee. We hadn't touched the pot from earlier that I made for Dylan, so I poured two cups and warmed them up in the microwave. I went to the fridge for the creamer and heard a door close. Maybe it was Dylan getting up in the other room.

Then my heart stopped. It wasn't a door closing inside the house. It was a car door and it was in the driveway. Quickly I glanced at the door and it was locked. My heart started racing. Was it Rachel? Michael?

Dylan emerged from my bedroom wearing jeans and no shirt, clearly having been woken up by the door outside.

"Is someone here?" he asked.

He could tell by the look of horror on my face that I was petrified to see who it was.

"Linds, relax. I got this."

"What if it's Michael? He will lose it if he sees you here." I was panicking and shaking.

Dylan came to me and put his hands on my arms to try and calm me. "Don't worry, nothing is going to happen to you. I'm here and I'm not going anywhere."

Immediately I could tell it was Michael when he started pounding on the front door, and I could tell by the tone of his voice without even comprehending the words that he was furious. Dylan's truck was in the driveway. Shit. That was the last thing on my mind when we came inside the night before. Never for a minute did I think he would be spending the night or that Michael would show up here to find his vehicle in the driveway.

I walked toward the door, still shaking and not sure what I was going to find on the other side when I opened it.

"Lindsey, just let him stay out there and pound on the door all day if he wants. You don't owe him any explanations, and I think you should let him cool off first."

Now he was pounding louder. "Open up this damn door, Lindsey! I know you're in there. Your car is in the garage. I wanna know who the hell is here. What the fuck is going on?"

I knew if I didn't deal with this now it would escalate and get out of hand.

My eyes welled with tears and I was now shivering. I was scared of Michael now. He hurt me last night worse than I ever thought possible, and I couldn't endure that pain again. The physical pain wasn't what hurt the most. It was the fact that I had loved him for so long and he had broken my heart and my trust. I knew things would never be the same with him even if I wanted to forgive him and try again. But the longer I let him stand outside practically breaking down the door, the worse it was going to get.

Dylan stepped in front of me. "Linds, you don't have to do this. Let me handle him." He reached into his bag on the floor by the couch, grabbed a t-shirt, and pulled it over his head.

He opened the door and the look on Michael's face said it all. Anger, confusion, hurt.

Michael knew Dylan from school and because he and my sister were so close. There was no reason to explain who he was, just why he was here.

Dylan spoke first, as I stood just behind him. "Beating down the door isn't going to get you anywhere. She doesn't want to see you."

Michael was fuming now, and I could tell this was going to escalate quickly. "What the hell are you doing here?"

He started to push his way past Dylan to get to me, but as expected he met resistance from Dylan. I retreated a little like a scared animal.

"Who the hell do you think you are? Get out of my way! Linds, we need to talk. Now."

Dylan pushed him back and he stumbled into the doorway. "I don't think you heard me, Michael. You're not coming in and she's not coming out."

"I think she can speak for herself. This has nothing to do with you, Dylan." Michael was not taking no for an answer. He never did.

I knew I would have to deal with Michael at some point, so I just wanted to get this over with now and move forward. I came out from behind my protector to face the music.

"Michael, please stop." I looked at Dylan, "It's okay, I can handle this. I think we have some things to discuss. I'll call you when we're done."

Dylan looked at me worryingly, "Lindsey, I'm not leaving you alone with him, not after what he did to you."

I knew the marks were on my neck and, with my hair pulled up and just a t-shirt on, I knew Michael could see them. He looked at me and I saw him deflate as he saw for the first time the hurt he had inflicted on me last night.

I touched my neck where the bruising was and lowered my head. I felt ashamed even though I knew this wasn't my fault. Making him mad was not a green light for him to lay his hands on me.

"Dylan, go inside and we will talk out here." I touched his hand and tried to look at him assuringly to let him know that I was okay.

He turned to walk inside, then looked back and addressed Michael. "I'll be inside. And I'm not going anywhere."

Michael didn't seem phased by Dylan's comment. The door closed behind Dylan and immediately Michael started in with me.

"First of all, what the hell is going on here? Why is he here?"

"I don't owe you any kind of explanation after the things you've done."

"Did they think you needed a bodyguard or something?" He was smirking and clearly not sorry at all for what he had done to me.

Apparently he thought what happened at the beach last night was some sort of joke.

"Is this funny to you, Michael?"

He pointed to the house and looked toward the window behind him, "They obviously thought that they needed to come here and protect you from 'big mean Michael', right?"

I could tell he thought Rachel was here too. Time for Michael to know what it feels like to be betrayed.

"What do you mean 'they'? Rachel isn't here."

And there it was. All of a sudden he was starting to process that there was more to this than he had thought when he first got here. He looked at my shirt and I think he instantly knew. The color left his face and he looked like he was in shock. "No. Lindsey, please tell me this isn't what it looks like."

I couldn't look at him, I just kept my head down as the tears started to fall. I didn't regret what happened with Dylan, but even though Michael had crushed me I still never wanted to hurt him. This wasn't how I wanted him to find out about what happened last night.

I wasn't going to back down and I certainly wasn't going to let him make me feel guilty after his indiscretions.

"Michael, if you want to talk about what happened between you and me, then we can talk. But Dylan is off limits. It's none of your business."

"Wow, that didn't take long. What did you wait, an hour or two?"

I wasn't going to let him make me feel bad for what happened with Dylan. "I said, we aren't discussing this. Honestly, Michael, I don't think there's anything for you and I to discuss at this point. We're done. What you did is unforgivable."

He stepped toward me reaching out for my arm and I wouldn't let him near me. I knew that if he touched me, Dylan would immediately be at my side and I didn't want a confrontation between the two of them.

"Linds, please talk to me. Let's work this out and try and move forward. I'm so sorry and I want to make it up to you. I promise it'll never happen again."

"Which part? The part where you tried to choke me or the part where you've been screwing someone else for the last year behind my back?"

He again reached for me and this time he grabbed my arm. It wasn't aggressive or forced at all, but the touch of his hand on my skin made me cringe. I immediately pulled away, and within seconds Dylan was at my side. I knew he would be watching from inside.

"You're done here, Michael. Don't lay another finger on her." Dylan was standing in front of me now between Michael and me.

Michael turned to leave, then stopped. "You'll regret this, Lindsey. I'm not going to wait for you."

"Wait for me? That's funny, Michael. You haven't waited for me all year while you were sleeping with Leslie." I couldn't believe he had the audacity to turn this around on me after everything he had done.

He glared at Dylan, and then smirked and said, "You can have her."

Part Two

"For every girl, there is a boy
she will never forget."
—unknown

Lindsey

$\mathcal{I}$f I would've known that would be the last time I saw Michael, maybe I would have stopped him from leaving. I could've tried to make him understand why Dylan was there and what had happened.

Everyone told me it wasn't my fault and that it was just an accident, but my heart felt something different. I knew that it wasn't even Michael that was at fault in the accident, but that was no comfort to me that he died thinking I had betrayed him.

Michael drove off that day furious and hurt beyond belief, and it was all because of me. When he left, Dylan and I went inside and he tried to tell me that Michael would be angry, but he would get over it. In that moment I knew he was right, but all of that would change when I got the call about the accident.

Michael was on his way back to the beach house in Galveston when he left my house that day. I didn't know this at the time, but it was discovered after the accident based on where it happened and after speaking to Mac who said Michael had called and said he was coming back. Mac told police investigators that Michael called around 7:30 P.M. to say that he was just leaving town and would be arriving around 8:30 or so that evening.

He had left my house around 3:15 P.M. but I had no idea where he had been for the four hours in between when he left here and called Mac. Later it would come out that he had gone to Leslie's house. She told police that he seemed "fine" and that they went for a drive and got something to eat. He dropped her back off at 7:15 P.M.

The fact that he left my house and went straight to her should've been enough to erase some of the guilt I felt, but it didn't.

According to the investigation, Michael was driving on Highway 59 when a car tried to merge into traffic from the left side of the highway at a turn-around. The driver claimed that the sun was glaring in her eyes and she didn't see his truck because of the glare.

Michael was unresponsive when paramedics and first responders got to the scene. A small, tiny piece of comfort in the entire excruciating ordeal would be that he didn't suffer. I did enough of that for both of us.

In a matter of twenty-four hours, my entire life and how I knew it had been completely shattered.

That day after he left, Dylan and I went inside the house and spent the rest of the afternoon trying to figure things out. Where did we go from here? How would we explain this to Melissa, Rachel…everyone?

We had just a few hours to try and start processing the newness of what had just happened between us when I got the call about Michael and the accident.

Dylan had gone to the store to pick up something to make for dinner. It had been a long twenty-four hours and we both decided we would stay in, have a nice dinner, and relax while we continued to figure things out. I had turned on some music and was lighting a few candles waiting for him to come back.

He brought steaks and all of the fixings for a Caesar salad. It felt so natural and easy being with him. We moved around the kitchen making the salad together like we had been doing this for years. He grabbed a beer for himself and a Diet Coke for me and we went onto the patio to grill the steaks.

My phone sat on the counter on silent to avoid any further calls or texts for the rest of the evening. I just wanted one night to forget about everything and try and focus on where to go from here.

We had dinner outside on the deck and stayed out there relaxing and talking until it became chilly and dark. Once inside, Dylan grabbed another beer from the fridge. As he was coming back from the kitchen to join me on the couch in the living room he noticed my phone had lit up with a call. It was from Michael's mom.

"Linds, Michael's mom is calling your phone." He walked into the living room and handed me the phone. It had already gone to voicemail.

I thought she would be most likely calling to find out what had been going on. She was the last person I wanted to talk to right now.

My phone notified me that I had a voicemail. I opened the voicemail tab and saw that I had four voicemails. There were seven missed calls and a number of texts too.

The missed calls were two from Michael's mom, one from Keri, one from Mac, two from Rachel, and one from a number I didn't recognize.

Suddenly I was worried.

I opened the voicemail from Keri first. I could tell she was crying. "Linds…call me right away…it's urgent. It's, um…just call me."

Then Mac, "I know Keri already left you a message, but you need to call one of us right away. Lindsey, call me. Please."

My first thought was that Michael had told them about Dylan and everyone was losing their minds over it. And if that was the case, now I really didn't want to hear what his mom had to say.

I deleted her voicemail without ever listening to it. Something I would later regret.

The last message I will never forget, it haunts me.

It was from the Harris County Sheriff's Department. "Ms. LaVere, this is Deputy Parker with the Harris County Sheriff's Department. We need to speak to you immediately. Please call the Department at 555-223-4360 and ask for me."

I had this terrible feeling in my stomach and I began to shake.

"Linds, what's going on?" Dylan could tell something was wrong and immediately was at my side.

"It was the sheriff's department. I have to call them back." I was dazed and shaken, completely caught off guard and startled. "I don't know what's going on, I don't know what to do and…" I couldn't catch my breath. I felt like someone was sitting on my chest cutting off my oxygen.

Dylan took the phone from my hand and replayed the voicemail. "Maybe it's nothing. Don't start jumping to conclusions and getting all worked up before we figure out what's happening. Do you want me to call?"

I couldn't speak, so I simply nodded my head and moved in close to him on the couch so I could hear the call.

The deputy came on the line and asked who he was speaking with and Dylan explained who he was and why he was calling. I began to hear words but I couldn't put them all together and process what was being said. "Michael…accident…ambulance…hospital…next of kin."

"Thank you, Deputy Parker. Yes, I will make sure to do that. Goodbye." Dylan ended the call and he was visibly shaken. He set my cell phone down on the table, turned toward me, and grabbed both of my hands in his. It took him a moment to look at me, and then he tried to speak.

"Linds, I, um…I'm not sure how to do this."

"Dylan, you're scaring me. What's wrong? Is it Rachel? Is it my…" he interrupted me.

"It's Michael. I don't know exactly what happened, but he was in an accident."

"Is he okay? I need to go to the hospital. Can you drive me? Wait, no, that'll make it worse. Did he say what hospital?" Dylan just stared at me not saying anything. "What's going on?"

"Lindsey, Michael isn't going to make it. He's on life support."

I could hear the words coming out of his mouth, but I wasn't comprehending what he was saying. There had to be some kind of mistake.

"I don't understand what you're saying." I could feel the room spinning, my heart racing, and it felt like I was going to pass out. "But he was just here. I—but I don't—no, there has to be a mistake!" Dylan was there, wrapping me up in his arms.

I don't remember much after that until we reached the hospital. On the way there Dylan was telling me what he was told by the deputy, but I was only hearing bits and pieces. Michael was on a life support machine for now and would be taken off of it as soon as his parents arrived back in town later this evening. They had been traveling to see friends in New Jersey and would fly home right away.

I was one of the ICE contacts on his phone, and that is why they contacted me. Later I would learn that Michael's mom called to tell me what happened and ask if I would stay with him at the hospital until they could get here. She undoubtedly had no idea that anything had happened between us, nor did she need to know at this point.

I knew that Mac and Keri were also on their way to the hospital, but they wouldn't be allowed to be with me while I sat by his side. Dylan insisted that he go inside with me and wait until they got there so I didn't have to be alone for this.

It was as if I was on autopilot walking through the parking garage, into the hospital, and then being led down the hallway to where he was. I don't even know if I was crying. I just felt numb…in shock.

100

Once we were inside Dylan led me to a registration area and he asked where we needed to go to find the ICU. We walked side by side through the hallways of the white, cold hospital, his hand on the small of my back as if to steady me. I remember that feeling of warmth from him, it was comforting and probably the only thing that helped get me through that dreadful time.

We reached another desk with a waiting area across from it and Dylan again went to the reception area and spoke to the nurses at the station. I sat down in a chair just inside the waiting area. I remember thinking, *Waiting area…waiting for news, good or bad…waiting to be told whether someone is going to live or die.* The named seemed appropriate and I was thankful my mind was wandering if only for a moment to escape what was happening around me.

Dylan came and stood in front of me. "Linds, the nurse will take you to see him, when you're ready."

I looked at him and thought about what he had just said. Would I ever be "ready" for this? How could anyone be "ready" to go and sit at the bedside of someone they loved and wait for them to die?

"I don't think I'll ever be ready to do this. It doesn't feel right, me being the one to sit with him after everything that's happened these past two days. I hurt him so bad. Maybe this is all my fault." The tears started to fall and I sobbed uncontrollably. Dylan wrapped his arms around me and I buried my head in his chest.

He let go and held me back, "Lindsey, you have to do this. He needs you to be with him. I will be right here when you need me. I'm not going anywhere. You can do this."

He leaned in, kissed me on the forehead and wiped the tears from my face.

I turned and let the nurse lead me through the doors into the ICU. When I reached the door to Michael's room, I could see him through the window lying there surrounded by machines. He looked like he had been in a fight, bruises and cuts on his face and his head was wrapped in a white bandage. There was a breathing tube in his mouth and tubes coming out of him everywhere.

The nurse told me that the doctor would be in to speak to me within the hour. She pulled a chair up to the side of his bed and said if I needed anything she would be out in the hall at the nurse's station.

What I needed, she couldn't give me.

I didn't know how to process what I was seeing. Michael was a strong, handsome, charismatic athlete but lying in that bed I didn't even recognize him. I sat down in the chair next to the bed. I wanted to touch his hand, put my head on his chest, and kiss his face.

Reluctantly, I reached for his hand. I don't know what I expected, but it was warm and soft and felt just like it normally did.

I laid my head on his chest and could feel the movement of his breathing, only it wasn't really his heart beating and his lungs breathing, it was just the machines. I closed my eyes and thought of all the times we had lay on the couch watching a movie, my head just like this on his chest. I thought of the times he had fallen asleep next to me and I could hear his heart beating. His eyes always opened eventually, but now they would forever stayed closed.

I wondered if he knew I was there, if he could feel my touch. No matter what we had been through recently, I loved him and I always would. The decision to no longer be with Michael was not up to me anymore…it had been made for me.

I'm not sure how much time passed while I lay there with him, but I was startled by the doctor's hand on my shoulder.

"Miss LaVere? Hi, I'm Dr. Grant. I know this is very difficult for you, but I want to give you an update on his condition."

"Ok, um thank you." I wiped the tears and tried to compose myself to hear what he was saying.

"Michael suffered severe head trauma from the impact of the crash. Paramedics performed CPR and did everything they could, but the damage was just too severe. When the ambulance arrived at the hospital, we continued life saving efforts and took him in for scans to assess the damage to the brain. The tests concluded that there was no brain activity. The sheriff deputy on the scene used Michael's phone to call the emergency contacts. They spoke to his parents and we were put in touch with them to discuss his condition and prognosis. His parents wanted him kept on life support until they could get here to," he paused, as if knowing that my heart was breaking as he was speaking. "…to sign the necessary paperwork and say goodbye. I'm so sorry, Miss LaVere. If there is anything we can do for you, please do not hesitate to ask."

He turned and walked out of the room, leaving me with Michael and all of those machines. It was overwhelming and I felt so alone sitting there with him.

As I held his hand I decided to say my goodbye to him while we were alone.

"Michael, um I, I don't know how to do this. I've said goodbye to you hundreds of times before, but I always knew I'd see you again later. I hate the way we left things, and I wish I had the chance to make you understand what was going on with me earlier today. Michael, you hurt me. You hurt me so badly. I don't know if I would've been able to forgive you, but I didn't want that to be the last time I saw you. I'm so sorry."

I didn't know if he could hear me or not, but I wanted to say the words out loud.

"Your parents are coming, and they want to say goodbye. I'll be with you until they get here. So I want to do this while it's just you and me. No matter what happens in the rest of my life, you will always be my first love. I want you to know that I will never forget you. Thank you for all of the wonderful things you've brought to my life. I love you, Michael."

Dylan

I could hardly believe what was happening all in a matter of twenty-four hours. The only thing I wanted was to make sure she was okay, and that he didn't come back to hurt her. Lindsey and I had made love, had an awkward confrontation with Michael, and now she was sitting at his bedside while he was dying. It was almost too much to process.

I took a seat in the waiting area after getting a cup of stale, lukewarm coffee from the cafeteria. So much had happened in the past twenty-four hours, it was just a lot to process.

All of a sudden, I realized I hadn't returned any of Melissa's calls or texts. By now she would no doubt be furious. I decided to text and then call her in the morning.

"Hey, I'm so sorry for not getting back to you today. You must be mad, and I don't blame you. There was an emergency with a friend from back home. I'm here helping out. I'll call you tomorrow." I paused for a second trying to decide how to end the text. I didn't want to raise any red flags so I finished with my typical, "love ya xoxo".

I felt some guilt about what happened with Lindsey last night, but on the other hand I didn't. I would talk to Melissa in person when we both got back into town. I wasn't sure what I would say or where things would go next for me, Lindsey, or Melissa.

And now that we were here, in this hospital, I had no idea what would happen next. Lindsey's entire world has been turned upside down and whatever she needs from me I will give her.

I couldn't imagine what she was feeling right now sitting next to him, watching and waiting for him to die. She shouldn't have to handle this by herself. Maybe I should call Rachel? I was afraid though if Rachel knew I was here she would start asking questions that Lindsey didn't need right now.

After a little while I heard someone asking where Michael was, and I recognized the voice. I turned to see Keri, Lindsey's best friend. I knew her from all of the time I spent with Rachel at her house, since Keri and Linds were joined at the hip since third grade.

I got up and walked toward her. She turned and recognized me instantly but still looked surprised to see me here.

"Dylan? What are you doing here?"

"Hey Keri." I stretched my hand out to her boyfriend, "Hi, I'm Dylan. I'm a friend of Lindsey's, well actually Rachel's, but I, uh…I brought Lindsey here. I was with her at her parents' house when she got the call from the sheriff's department."

They both seemed confused, but I'm sure that wasn't their number one concern right now either.

"Hey, I'm Mac. Where's Linds? Is she with Mike?"

"Yeah, the nurses took her back to sit with him in ICU. His parents are out of town I guess and are flying in around 1 A.M. They asked Lindsey to sit with him until they could get here to say good…I mean, um, so that someone was with him." I knew that Michael was their best friend and this was devastating for them, so I tried to be as kind as can be. I was still furious with him for what he did to Lindsey last night, but that was insignificant now considering the circumstances.

Just then, Lindsey appeared from around the hallway corner. She wasn't crying anymore. She just looked pale and numb, almost as if she was sleepwalking.

Keri turned and ran to her, "Oh Lindsey, I'm so sorry! What can we do? What did the doctors say?"

She looked at me and started to cry, so I spoke up to save her from going through it again.

"Michael was severely injured in the accident. They did all they could to save him, but the damage to his brain was too massive. They have him on life support until his parents can get here to make the final decision. I'm so sorry, I know how close all of you were, I mean are."

Mac spoke up, "He is an organ donor."

Lindsey turned and looked at him, puzzled. "What did you say?"

"He's an organ donor. I know because we got our licenses together and we both checked the box that says organ donor."

Keri quickly chimed in, "Mac, don't you think that it's a little early to start talking about that?"

"No, no, I'm glad he said something." Lindsey seemed almost herself for a moment. "Maybe something good can come of this. I wonder if the doctor's know, or if his parents even know."

I was going to take the opportunity to leave for a minute, so I piped up and announced that I would check with the nurse to be sure they had read his license that he was a donor.

This situation was excruciating enough for the three of them, and I shouldn't even be here anymore. I wanted to be here for Lindsey, but this was something that I think she probably wanted to do on her own. My being here would only complicate things and raise questions that didn't need to be asked at the present time.

I spoke to the head nurse and she informed me that yes, they had checked to see if he was a donor, but that they could only discuss that with his next of kin.

The three of them were huddled together in a row of chairs when I came back into the waiting area. "Can I get anyone a coffee or anything?"

Mac stood up, "What did they say? Do they know about Mike being an organ donor?"

"Yes, but they will only discuss that with his parents." I looked at Lindsey to catch her eye. "Hey Linds, can I talk to you for a sec in the hall?"

We moved into the hallway and I wanted so badly to hold her. Out of the corner of my eye I could see Keri and Mac burning holes through me staring, waiting to see what was going on.

"Lindsey, I really think it would be best if I go now. Your friends are here and Michael's parents will be here in just a few hours. I don't want this to get complicated for you right now. This is more important. Are you okay with me going?"

She looked at me, her eyes piercingly green, like they got when she cried. "I need you, but I also know you should go. It doesn't feel right you being here, and I don't want to have to explain this to anyone right now."

"I want to hold you and tell you everything is going to be okay." I had to fight the urge to wrap her up in my arms and not let go. "I'll go back to your house and straighten things up before I head back to school. If you need me, just call or text and I'll come right back."

She smiled at me and leaned in to put her head on my chest. Her arms wrapped around me and I could feel her sobbing cries through her body. I held her for a few minutes, and tried to reassure her that it would all be okay. I didn't care that she was crying for someone else because all I knew was that she hurt, so I hurt.

I kissed her on the forehead, and then on that tiny little freckle on the tip of her nose.

"I'll check in with you soon."

Then I turned to leave. I could hear her crying as I walked down the hall. I wanted to turn around and scoop her up in my arms, but I knew I had to go. Just before I reached the door I turned to see her one more time. Keri had gone to her and was hugging her now. She was being taken care of, and that was all that mattered to me at that moment.

If I had known how things would unfold in the days to come, I'm not sure I would've left Lindsey's side at the hospital. Maybe it wouldn't have made a difference, but at least I would've had a little more time with her.

I drove to her house in a fog trying to process what was happening. Even with all that had taken place between her and Michael in the last twenty-four hours, or the last year for that matter, she loved him and this was going to crush her world. Life wouldn't be the same for her for a very long time, if ever. Selfishly I worried about how this would affect our situation and where we would go from here. I wanted to explore the possibility of a relationship with Lindsey, despite the age difference. She would be graduating this year and had turned eighteen a month ago, so the difference in our ages wasn't that alarming.

Obviously there was Melissa to consider, and I definitely wanted to make sure that I handled the break-up with her gently and respectfully. The fact that I had sex with Lindsey last night was wrong, and I knew it. I wouldn't let that happen again until things with Melissa were over.

I got back to Lindsey's house and picked up the kitchen and living room. It was after midnight at this point and my options for sleeping were limited. I wasn't going to drive the two hours back to my apartment and I didn't want to wake my mother this late by showing up at her house. My best option was to just sleep on the couch here and leave for home early in the morning.

I wanted to be home when Melissa got back from her trip so I could talk to her right away and not prolong this conversation about our future. I still wasn't sure if my future was with Lindsey, but either way I felt as though I needed to let Melissa go so she could find someone to love her the way she deserved to be loved.

Melissa

That last trip with Kyle had made me realize that it was time to make a decision and choose one of them. I loved them both. I had recently read a quote that really got me thinking and questioning my relationship with Dylan.

"If you love two people at the same time, pick the second one. If you really loved the first one, you wouldn't have fallen for the second."

As profound as this was, it didn't help with the fact that I had wanted a life with Dylan for so long that I couldn't really see myself with anyone else. At least until I met Kyle.

Kyle and I were away that week and the guilt was starting to eat away at me. My head told me that being with Kyle would be a good, safe choice. He was grounded and stable and knew that he wanted a future with me including marriage, kids, and the white picket fence. Dylan on the other hand was what my heart wanted. I had no idea what my future would be like if I stayed with Dylan. He showed no interest in wanting to get married, and had just recently started talking about moving in together.

I knew that before I moved in with him I would have to figure things out. He had been talking about it for a few months and instead of him being the one dragging his feet, now it was me.

We had set up appointments to look at townhomes and twice I had cancelled. Next week we were set to look again and Dylan was anxious to pick one since his lease with his current roommates was up in a month.

Before Kyle and I left wine country to head back to Austin, we had a sunset dinner at the resort our last night there.

I spent longer in the shower than usual, just trying to clear my head and make some sense of what I was doing. When I toweled off, I looked around the room and Kyle was nowhere to be found. However, on the bed was a single white rose and a note. The note read:

Liss,
Take your time getting ready. I have a surprise for you…text me when you're done and I'll come up and get you.
Love,
Kyle

He was always doing things like this for me, the hopeless romantic that he was. I loved this about him. He had the ability to make me feel like I was the only woman in the world.

I slipped into the silver satin dress that I had brought with me, hoping I would need it for a special evening with him. The matching thong and lace bra underneath would be an extra touch that he would no doubt love seeing after dinner.

As I applied my make-up and dried and straightened my hair, I couldn't help but wonder where Dylan was and what he was doing. I knew he was playing cards the night before at Rachel and Todd's, but we had been playing phone tag since then.

Knowing that Kyle had something in store for tonight, I thought I would text Dylan now and let him know that I'd call him tomorrow once I got to the airport to head home. The last message I had received from him was late last night saying that he had gone back home to help a friend with an emergency. I didn't respond last night, but I sent him a text this morning saying, "Got your message just now. Hope all is okay. Call me later. Xoxo."

I never heard from him though. Should I be worried? He said a friend had an emergency but he didn't say who.

"Hey, I never heard from you today. Hope all is okay with your friend. The girls and I are heading out for dinner and our last night on the town. Call you tomorrow from the airport. Can't wait to see you. Xoxo."

Most of that was true. I was missing him, even though I was having an amazing time with Kyle. My heart was still with Dylan.

I knew what I had to do, and I felt guilty being here with Kyle this week when I knew I'd have to end things with him. Selfishly I guess I just wanted a little more time.

When I got back I would commit completely to Dylan and to starting our life together. We'll pick out a townhome and begin moving forward which is what I had always wanted, until Kyle came along.

I wanted to enjoy this last evening with Kyle and I would wait until we got back to tell him it was over. Looking back on it, I was disgusted with myself for not telling him sooner. It wasn't fair to him.

Once I was ready I sent Kyle a text and he appeared at the door in a few minutes. He looked amazing as usual. Kyle had that polished good guy look with sandy blonde hair, blue eyes, and a perfect smile. He was tall and lean, and he exuded confidence, but not arrogance.

When he opened the door, he immediately smiled at me, "Wow, you look amazing tonight. And that dress…"

I blushed a little, something he always could make do with his charm and compliments. Unlike Dylan, Kyle's affection and flattery never sounded rehearsed or motivated. Dylan flirted with every woman he came in contact with, so his words of praise usually lost their meaning with me.

I smiled and kissed him on the cheek, "So what's the surprise you've got for me tonight?"

"Patience my dear, first dinner."

He held out his hand and waited for mine. I let him lead me through the resort, and as we passed the restaurant I wondered where we were having dinner. We kept walking down the pathway through the gardens and out toward the vineyards.

"Kyle, where are you taking me?" I was giddy with excitement and wonder. He was always doing things like this that were spontaneous and romantic.

"You'll see," he smiled. "Just a little further."

We eventually came to the end of the pathway and suddenly we were on the edge of a hillside looking over the valley below us. The sun was just beginning to set, and in front of us was a table set for two with candles, white linens, and flowers.

"Oh my gosh, Kyle. I've never seen anything so beautiful!" I was in pure amazement of the setting in front of me. It was like a scene from a romantic movie laid out before my eyes.

"Neither have I." He was looking at me and I knew he wasn't referring to the dinner table.

Tears filled my eyes, as I thought about how badly I was going to hurt him in just a few short days. At this moment I wanted to change my mind and choose him, but I knew that my heart would always belong to Dylan.

He turned to me and saw that I was on the verge of tears. "What's wrong?"

I played it off. "It's just so beautiful. I can't believe you did all this for me."

He took my hand and led me to the table, pulling my chair out for me to be seated. Within seconds, two waiters appeared and poured champagne for us both and started our dinner with an appetizer of shrimp cocktail. As we continued to eat course after course, there was soft music playing, and the sun was nearing its departure for the day.

"Kyle this is the most amazing surprise. I love it."

"The night isn't over yet," he smiled. "Maybe this isn't even the surprise."

I knew I had to be blushing again because I could feel the warmth in my cheeks. The champagne wasn't helping either, as I was started to get a little tipsy.

We finished our dinner and were served a deliciously decadent triple-chocolate cake for dessert and coffee with Bailey's and whipped cream.

The sun had set, and we were suddenly surrounded by thousands of little white lights and candles. I must've gotten lost in the conversation with Kyle because I hadn't even noticed the transition.

That was always one of the things I loved about being with Kyle. Time seemed to stand still for me when we were together. We had effortless conversations and could sit for hours with no awkward silences just being with one another.

There had not been much conversation during dinner tonight, and I hoped that he didn't notice how quiet I was being. My mind was spinning with thoughts of how I was going to have to tell him we were over.

He stood up and extended his hand to me.

"Dance with me?"

All of a sudden I heard the music clearly. I smiled hearing the soft beginning of "Into the Mystic", the song that he knew was my favorite. We had danced to this in my apartment one night a few months ago.

"I'd love to," I smiled and took his hand, once again letting him lead the way. I never had to be the lead when I was with Kyle. He took initiative and was a planner. Dylan would always just say, "Whatever you want to do" and I'd have to make all the arrangements, no matter how big or small.

He held me tight as we danced slowly under the stars that were now starting to make their appearance in the clear night sky. I closed my eyes and breathed in the smell of him, a familiar place I would not be able to escape to any longer.

The song had stopped yet we were still holding each other and moving to our own music. I wanted to stay here in his arms and not return to the reality that awaited me.

Kyle lifted my chin, touched the side of my face, and kissed me gently on my lips. He lingered for a few seconds before opening his eyes to look at me.

"Melissa, I love you. I've known it for awhile now, but I didn't want to complicate things more for you. I don't expect you to say it back, but I wanted you to know how I feel about you. I want a life with you. I want more than this sneaking around and getting you when you can get away."

I didn't know what to say. I knew I loved him too, but if I said it, it would make it harder for him when I ended it. God, I felt like the most horrible person right now!

"Kyle, I—I don't know what to say."

He reached down to hold my hands, "You don't have to say anything. That's not why I said it." He took a small step back from me and let go of my hands, reached into his pocket, and before I knew what was happening he was lowering himself to one knee.

My head was spinning. Was he really going to propose to me?!?

"Melissa, we are perfect together in every way and I want to share my life with you. I know you can't answer me now, but take some time and think about your answer. Marry me?"

He opened the ring box and a spectacular princess cut diamond was gleaming at me from inside.

"Kyle, it's beautiful." I began to cry. "I don't know what to say."

"I told you I don't expect an answer now. I want you to think about it, think about what kind of life we could have together."

I couldn't look at him for fear he would be able to see my answer written all over my face. I was going to wait until we got back from the trip, but since the opportunity had presented itself, I couldn't help but think this was the time. The last thing I wanted to do was to spoil this amazing trip, but I needed to do this.

"Kyle, there's something I need to tell you. I've been doing a lot of thinking about what I want in my life, and I know I need to make a decision. I know that you and I would have an amazing life together, and if the timing was different I would say 'yes' to you a million times over. But Dylan and I have years together and I just can't walk away from that history I have with him. I'm sorry, Kyle, but my answer today is no and it won't change tomorrow, or the day after that."

I could tell this was killing him, and my heart was breaking not just for him but for me too since I really did love him.

He closed the ring box and put it back in his pocket. I tried to reach for his hand and he turned to walk away from me.

"Kyle, I'm so sorry. I was going to wait and figure this out when we got back in town. I wanted to enjoy our time away and not think about any of this, but when you proposed it just all became very clear to me."

And then it was as if I struck a nerve with something I had said because he stopped and turned toward me, "So you knew already that you were going to choose him?" Now he looked hurt and angry. Kyle never got mad about anything, but now he looked like someone had struck him in the face. "You let me take you away, treat you like a queen, and even propose to you…but you had no intentions of seeing me anymore?"

I realized that what I said had come out wrong. It wasn't completely untrue, but once I had said it I realized how awful it sounded.

"I didn't realize how that came out until I heard myself say it. I'm sorry. I wish I could explain what is going on in my head, but I can't."

We sat down at the table, both clearly upset. I knew I had just crushed him, and it was the hardest thing I'd ever had to do.

"Liss, you should've told me before we came on this trip together if you already knew how you felt." His tone was sharp but also broken in a sad way.

"Until the moment that you pulled out that ring, I wasn't totally sure of what to do. That's the most honest answer I can give you. Something inside me just told me it was wrong and that I couldn't say yes to you." I paused, waiting for the right words to come to me. "If I couldn't say yes immediately then I feel like that's my answer now," I paused, "and always."

After a few minutes of awkward silence he finally spoke. "Well, we can do one of two things…one of us can take the next flight home and we can end this right here, right now." Then he stood and reached for my hand, ever the gentleman. "Or we can spend our last night together here and make it spectacular. I know what my choice is, but I'll leave it up to you."

I didn't say anything, I didn't need to. I took his hand and we danced a little longer. We didn't speak again until we got back to the room.

We both knew this would be the last time we would be together, so we made every moment last.

It was hard to wake up and look at him the next morning knowing that I wouldn't be in his arms again. I knew it was the right decision, but it still didn't make it any easier. His heart was breaking. My heart was breaking.

I lay quiet for almost an hour just watching him sleep. This man was exactly what I needed in my life these past few months. My only regret was hurting him. He deserved much more than this. I knew that I had to let him go so he could find someone that would fully give her heart to him because he shouldn't settle for anything less.

I nestled my face into the crease of his neck and shoulder and just took him all in. The scent of him was intoxicating and I wondered if I would always remember this feeling or if slowly it would fade from my memory.

A tear came down the side of my face and landed on his skin. He woke and raised his head to turn and look at me with those gorgeous cornflower blue eyes of his.

He smiled, kissed my cheek, "Liss, everything will work out exactly how it's supposed to. If we're meant to be, then we will find our way back to each other. I love you enough to let you go and figure out where your future is going to lead you."

"I don't deserve you, Kyle." I began to cry again and as I did he held me.

"Melissa, it's not about 'deserving' someone. It's just not our time, I guess."

I knew he was right, but my heart still ached inside for what could've been between us. My heart wanted Dylan and it wasn't fair for me to keep delaying the inevitable.

It was 8:05 A.M. and check-out wasn't until eleven so we lay there in bed just silent in each other's arms for awhile. Kyle ordered coffee and bagels from room service while I showered.

As I let the hot water wash over me, I closed my eyes and thought about life without him now. No more romantic getaways, slow dancing in the living room of my apartment in the middle of the night, or picnics in the park at our favorite little hideaway spot on the bluff.

I had gotten lost in my thoughts and didn't hear him come into the shower. His lips brushed against the skin of my shoulder while his arms gently encased my body from behind. No words, just silence between us as we continued to take in each last moment together.

We toweled off and sat in our luxurious white robes enjoying our coffee and bagels on the balcony. Soon we would be heading to the airport for our quick, but no doubt longer and more somber, flight back to reality.

As we both dressed and packed to leave, the silence was evident. We both busied ourselves awkwardly making small talk with each other until we were both ready to check out.

The shuttle ride to the airport was completely silent. He held my hand and we both just quietly stared out the window. I wondered if he was thinking and feeling what I was…wishing that this ride to the airport and plane ride would go on forever so that we didn't have to say our final goodbye.

He squeezed my hand and I turned to look at him. There were tears in my eyes that I tried to hold back unsuccessfully.

"I love you too, Kyle." I lowered my head and the tears came faster. "I really do love you. I'm just so sorry."

He wrapped me in his arms and I could feel his staggered breathing and I knew he was fighting back his emotions.

The driver made an announcement for gate departures, so I dried my eyes and we collected ourselves and belongings and readied for our stop at Gate B.

I was emotionally exhausted and slept the entire plane ride, which at the time I was thankful for, but looking back I wish I would've been awake for every last moment with him.

The plane landed and once we left the baggage claim, we headed to the terminal where we would separate one last time, as we had driven our own vehicles and met at the airport for the beginning of the trip.

"I'll walk you to your car." He held my hand as we passed through the airport. We normally were so careful about anyone seeing us together, but in that moment no one existed except the two of us. This was about us, and our last moments together.

He loaded my bags into my car and turned to me and smiled, "I just want you to be happy, even if it's not with me."

"I know, Kyle, and I want that for you too. Thank you for the most amazing trip."

We held onto each other for awhile, not wanting to move. I knew I would see him at the hospital, but things would be different now.

He kissed me, and we lingered there on each other's lips for a few moments. And then, it was over.

I drove home physically and emotionally exhausted. Once I got to my apartment, I was relieved that my roommate was not home. It gave me a chance to unpack, have a cup of coffee, put on some comfy clothes and start to figure out where to go from here.

Dylan would most likely be home by now, so I decided to text him and let him know I was home.

"Hey D. Just got home. In my comfy clothes on the couch. Fresh coffee on. U home? If so, join me. Xoxo."

My message showed he had read it, and he was typing me back a text. I waited, but nothing came through. Maybe he was still driving home and out of range for service. I turned the television on and got snuggled in on the couch. He would most likely come over once he got my text.

Lindsey

The hours felt more like days as I sat by Michael's side while he lay motionless in that cold hospital bed. I watched as the machines kept his heart beating and all I could do was wish for one more minute with him. One more chance to tell him that I love him, and that I always would. He had hurt me more than I could've ever imagined, but that would not erase all of the wonderful memories spent together.

All of the major "firsts" in my life up until this point belonged to Michael. He asked me out on my first official date when I was just fourteen, too young for a date according to my parents, even though it was just a PG-13 movie and fries and milkshakes at the mall. My first homecoming dance, first kiss, and eventually after waiting two years until I was almost seventeen, I lost my virginity to Michael.

He knew how important it was to me and he made it special. After a Friday night football game, we drove out to his grandparents' horse ranch for a picnic under the stars. He had a cooler with chocolate covered strawberries, cheese and crackers, and sparkling cider. It was still warm enough, but there was a slight chill in the air. Michael laid out several blankets and pillows, a Coleman camping lantern and a small radio. I had told my parents I was staying at Keri's for the night, and because I knew they were so used to me being at her house, they wouldn't check up on me.

We lay underneath the stars fumbling our way around this new experience together. It was his first time as well, so it made us both more relaxed that there were no expectations from each other. I'm not sure that it was all that we had built it up in our minds to be, but nevertheless, it was a night that neither of us would ever forget.

As I sat there with my head on his chest listening to his breath, I closed my eyes and drifted back to that moment after we first made love. I was resting my head on his chest and he was lying there with his arms wrapped tightly around me snuggled under a mound of blankets. He told me he loved me and he always would. In that moment I believed him.

Michael's parents arrived and things began to swirl around me. His mother was crying and his father was demanding answers from anyone that would listen to his questions.

I snuck quietly and indiscreetly out of the room and went to the waiting area hoping that Keri and Mac would still be there. Keri was there, laying across two chairs curled up with her head on what looked like Mac's letterman jacket, eyes closed sleeping.

I sat on the chair next to her, rested my head in my hands and quietly cried. I was so exhausted from the last forty-eight hours. All I wanted was to go home and sleep and just wake up from this nightmare.

Mac must have gone to the cafeteria because he returned with a coke and some snacks from the vending machine. "Linds, do you want something to eat?"

"No, thanks. I'm not hungry. I'm just so tired."

He came over and sat down two chairs away from me. He opened his arms and ushered me in to put my head on his lap. "Close your eyes for a little while, Linds. I'll wake you if there's any news."

I gladly took the opportunity to rest my swollen achy eyes and was thankful for these two amazing friends sitting here with me. Mac was like a brother to Michael and also one of my best friends all throughout school. Unfortunately for Mac, he knew all too well what it felt like to lose someone you loved in an accident.

Just two years ago, his older brother Stephen was killed in an accident just a few miles from his house. He and some friends left a party to go to a convenient store and buy cigarettes and snuff. They were all killed instantly, as the vehicle they were driving turned into the path of a tractor trailer that couldn't stop in time to avoid hitting them. Stephen wasn't driving, but he was ejected from the vehicle and later died from massive internal injuries at the hospital.

When the doctors told Mac's family that Stephen wasn't going to pull through, they inquired unselfishly about organ donation. Stephen had in fact, according to his driver's license, chosen to be a donor.

Mac's family took comfort in the fact that while they had to say goodbye to their son and brother, he would be saving the lives of many other sons and daughters, brothers and sisters by choosing to be an organ donor. Mac was always very proud of his brother and looked up to him as a role model.

This must've been why Mac was so vocal about Michael being an organ donor. I was so consumed with my own pain and what was happening that I never stopped to think about how this was going to hit home with him.

I lifted my head and looked up at him. Tears were slowly and silently streaming down his face as he stared at the blank wall in front of him.

"Mac?" I spoke quietly not wanting to wake Keri next to us. "Are you thinking about your brother?"

He didn't speak, he simply nodded his head and tried to blink away the tears. I didn't want to push but wanted him to know that I cared.

His idol, his hero, his brother was gone and now the closest person he had to a brother was slipping away too. I couldn't imagine the toll this would take on him and how it would affect his life.

"I tried to make sense of it when Stephen died, and I thought that if he could help others by saving a life then it would mean something. But it didn't. It didn't change the fact that my brother was still gone. And now Michael?" He was losing his composure now. I sat up and slid into the seat next to him wrapping my arms around his chest. "Linds, I can't lose him too."

"I know, Mac. It's not fair." I tried to be strong for him, but this was killing me too. I had never suffered a loss like this so I was just beginning to know the pain that he had been dealing with past two years. And now that he had to go through it all over again, he was right, it wasn't fair. As much as my heart was breaking for what I lost, it was also hurting for Mac. This would be a devastating loss for not just our group of friends and Michael's family, but for an entire community.

We sat in silence for another hour or so until Michael's parents came out to the waiting room to update us. By then Trisha and Chris had come to sit with us and wait to hear the outcome.

Michael's father spoke while his mother sat between Mac and I and held our hands. "You kids are Michael's family. We're glad you're all here for him and for us. The doctors have told us we have just a few hours before we need to let him go. Mac, as you know, Michael wanted to be an organ donor. I think that was because of you and Stephen. I'm proud of him, and you, for making that decision. We are going to lose our son, your friend, but someone else is going to be able to have theirs because of Michael."

He walked over and stood in front of Mac, stretched out his hand. "Thank you, son." Mac stood and embraced Mr. Stevenson and he finally let go of the emotion he had been trying to hold back.

Over the next hour, we all cried and held each other trying to just survive. The doctor came out around 4 A.M. and announced that preparations were ready to remove Michael from the life support machines and begin the organ donation procedure. Without saying the words, we knew what he meant. It was time to start saying goodbye to Michael.

I was thankful for the time I had with Michael earlier before everyone else had arrived. My goodbye to him was private and I was selfishly glad that I was able to be alone with him tonight.

Trisha, Keri, and Chris all went in together and as expected, both girls were beyond upset when they emerged from his room. Chris held both of them under his arms and announced that he would drive them home. We all embraced as a group, and Mac and I stayed behind.

I knew Mac would want some time alone to say his goodbye to Michael.

"Mac, I can stay and wait for you, if you want."

He stood frozen, staring down the hallway toward the room where his best friend was being kept alive by machines. "I don't know how to do this, Linds. I just—can't do this again."

I walked toward him and grabbed his hands. "You can do this, I know you can. If you don't, you will regret it forever."

"Will you come with me?"

He had suddenly turned from a strong, athletic eighteen-year-old man into a broken, young boy. I knew that this was going to hit him hard because of his brother's recent passing.

I latched my left arm into his right and rested my head on his arm. Our friendship went beyond the fact that he was Michael's best friend. We were friends long before that, and would no doubt be friends for a long time to come.

"I'll be here as long as you need me. Right here, by your side."

We slowly walked down the hall to Michael's room, two young people about to have both their hearts shattered by the most unfortunate accident.

I sat with Mac while he struggled to find the words to say goodbye to Michael. We cried together while we both prayed over him, each holding one of his hands and each other's. It was hard to know when it was time to let go.

As much as we wanted to stay with him forever, we knew that his parents needed to be here with him for his final moments. Mac squeezed his hand and told him goodbye and walked toward the door where he stood and waited for me.

I kissed Michael on the forehead, then on his lips softly while I held his hand. The tears rolled down my face falling onto his cheek. I watched my tears slide down his face, and I wondered if he could feel them. I hoped in that moment that he knew what he had meant to me and how much I loved him. I always would.

Mac nestled me under his arm while we walked away from Michael for the last time. I felt numb from the last twenty-four hours of emotional hell.

"Come on, Linds, I'll drive you home."

Suddenly I remembered…Dylan. He had left the hospital about four hours ago to go back to my house and clean up. I had no idea if he was staying there or if he had gone back to College Station. There was no way I wanted to explain this to Mac, not tonight at least.

"I can't go home, I don't want to be alone right now." I had hoped that Mac would easily pick up on what I was saying.

"I'm sorry, I didn't even think about it. Do you want me to take you to Keri's house, or you can just come back to my house and hang with me? No one is there either, and I guess I really don't want to be there by myself. So we could, I don't know, lean on each other for awhile."

His arm was still draped around my shoulder, and right then it felt like the safest place I could be.

"Yeah, I'd really like that Mac. Thanks."

I was thankful for the bond that he and I had throughout the past ten years and knew that he was too. We had a tight group of friends, but the two of us were definitely the closest to Michael and would feel this loss the hardest.

The fifteen-minute drive to his house was silent, with only a few words spoken between us. Once at his house, he found a pair of sweats and a t-shirt for me to put on and although they were grossly oversized for me I was still the most comfortable I had been all night. He grabbed me a couple blankets and a pillow and helped me settle in on the couch before he went to shower and change.

I was exhausted, but my mind was swirling. I tried closing my eyes hoping that I could simply doze off eventually. Thoughts of Michael and Dylan both filled my head. Just a few hours ago I was ready to move forward, without Michael, but not like this. All I wanted was a clean break from the turbulent relationship that we were stuck in. And now, he was gone forever.

It was impossible for me to think about moving forward now. I had no idea how I was going to process the fact that Michael was gone.

Looking back on this day, I would always know that this was the day that forever changed my life.

Dylan

As much as I wanted to stay in town and be there for Lindsey, I knew this wasn't something I could do for her. The best thing I could do would be to go back home and give her the space she needed to grieve this loss and start to move on.

The two-hour drive home felt like an eternity as my mind swirled with thoughts of what she must be going through and how hurt she must be. I'd check in on her as soon as I got home and let her know that I would do whatever I could for her.

I thought about Melissa on the way home as well. I knew that I would need to figure out how to tell her that it was time for us to admit that we just weren't working. Even despite what had happened with Lindsey, I knew that Melissa just wasn't right for me. We were supposed to look at townhouses this week and move in together soon. My lease with my roommates was up soon and Melissa had always been pushing for us to move in together so I thought this would be a good time for us to give it a try.

I decided to go home first and shower and clear my head a little before I talked to Melissa. I wanted to make sure Lindsey was doing okay and that she wasn't dealing with this on her own.

Once I got to my apartment I showered and texted Lindsey. No reply. It was almost noon and I wondered if maybe she was sleeping. Most likely she was up all night at the hospital, and I had been at her house until seven in the morning in case she came home but she didn't.

I was exhausted so I decided to go to bed for awhile. Melissa's plane wouldn't be in for a few more hours, so I figured I would get some sleep.

Sleep came easy for me after being up late the last two nights, and I was startled awake by an incoming text on my phone. Hoping it was Lindsey, I quickly reached for it to see. It was Melissa. She was boarding the plane and would let me know when she was home. I tried to drift off again, but closing my eyes didn't help. I still couldn't get Lindsey off my mind. I decided to send her a text and see if she was okay.

"Hey Linds. Just wanted to check and see how you are doing."

She replied immediately, "I'm okay. Well, I'm not, but how can I be?"

My heart hurt for her, and all I wanted to do was wrap her up in my arms and tell her everything would be alright someday. "Tell me what I can do."

This time her reply didn't come so quickly. I didn't want to pressure her or overstep, but I wanted her to know that if she wanted me then I was in this one hundred percent.

When she finally texted back I could tell that she was preoccupied and talking about the two of us was the furthest thing from her mind. "I'm just trying to wrap my head around everything. I don't know how to get through this."

I knew she was referring to Michael, not me. I had to let her grieve and deal with his death and not complicate things for her.

"Linds, I think you should just take your time and let yourself grieve." I paused, wondering if I should say anything about us or if I should just let it go for now. "If you want to talk, I'm here."

Her reply was short and sweet. "Thank you."

That would be the last time she and I would have any communication for a very long time.

I'm not sure if our signals got crossed, or whether I should've made more of an effort to reach out to her. I wanted to give her space to deal with Michael's death and I was going to wait for her to come to me when she was ready. But weeks would pass with no word from her.

The next day I went to see Melissa with my best game face on. I knew that I needed to figure out a way to move past the events of the past two days and let myself fall back into my life with her.

I let myself into her apartment that she shared with her roommate, and she was asleep on the couch. On my way, I stopped to grab her favorite mocha latte from Starbucks as I usually did.

I set our coffees down on the coffee table and gently slid onto the couch, trying not to wake her. She stirred as I nestled my arm under her head and placed it on my chest. She buried her head into my shirt and inhaled deeply, smiling as she recognized the smell of my cologne. Her arms wrapped around me tightly and I stroked her hair as she started to fall back to sleep.

I thought of Lindsey and how I had held her like this just yesterday comforting her. For now, I knew I had to give her the space and time she needed to grieve.

One month following my return home, Melissa and I were supposed to sign a lease on a townhouse together, a huge step for our relationship. I couldn't bring myself to do it though. I knew deep inside that a piece of my heart would always be with Lindsey, but my head told me that the best thing to do would be to let her go. Our lives were too different and the timing was just wrong for us both.

I wondered at the time if Melissa could tell that something was going on with me because she seemed to be very distant. She didn't seem to mind that I had changed my mind about the townhouse, in fact she seemed almost relieved.

Melissa

I hated to say I was relieved that Dylan had changed his mind about moving in together but I was. At the time, I never questioned him about it because I was preoccupied with what happened recently with Kyle, and I was thankful that whatever was going on with him had kept him from noticing that I wasn't myself.

The weeks following my trip with Kyle were brutal and had been the hardest of my life so far. Ending things with Kyle was painful for me, as I genuinely had deep real feelings for him. Walking away from someone that I knew wanted to give me the world was a risk I was willing to take because I loved Dylan and desperately wanted a future with him.

That Sunday afternoon when I got home from my trip with Kyle, I settled in on the couch expecting Dylan would come by on his way back from helping whichever friend had been in need over the weekend. Instead, I had fallen asleep waiting for him. I woke in the morning to the intoxicating smell of him as he settled in on the couch with me.

I was awake but kept my eyes closed, trying to enjoy the moment with him. This was where I needed to be. I had been derailed these past few months with the newness and excitement of the attention and lavish spoiling that I received from Kyle. Dylan wasn't the guy that did those kinds of things. His idea of romance was putting the toilet seat down so that I wouldn't fall in. But he also did little things for me that I stopped noticing because I was focused on being pampered by another man.

He would always do the dishes if I cooked a meal for us. "You make the mess, I'll do the rest." That was our standing agreement. When there was anything

131

that needed fixing in my apartment, he was always there to help. Dylan never whisked me away to wine country on a spur of the moment trip, but he was always there for me when I truly needed him.

I was an idiot. All men did those things in the beginning of a relationship, and eventually they tapered off and settled in. Men 101. Now that's the kind of class that should be taught to all women looking to fall in love!

And here he was now, giving me exactly what I needed. His arms were wrapped around me, and in addition to his cologne that he knew was my favorite, I smelled a hot mocha latte nearby.

"Good morning, handsome." I snuggled into him and nuzzled at his neck.

He squeezed me tight. "I didn't want to wake you. I missed you." He kissed my forehead and continued stroking my hair.

I wanted to tell him that I missed him and that I was happy to be back. I'd be lying if I did though. Truth is, I did miss him, but I was thinking about Kyle and feeling guilty for hurting him. My guilt about being unfaithful to Dylan was starting to surface as well. I loved Dylan, and the last thing I wanted to do was to hurt him. After what I had done, I could only hope that he would never find out and that I could just move past it. I loved him, and I wanted a life with him.

I knew it was going to take time to get past what happened with Kyle, but the fact that my clinicals were almost over for the semester would help tremendously.

Now that I had graduated, I could start applying for jobs at other hospitals. I knew that I couldn't stay where I was now because it wasn't fair to either of us. Kyle needed to be able to move on and he wouldn't be able to do that with me around all of the time.

Suddenly it dawned on me that I had no idea what Dylan had been doing all weekend back in Katy.

I sat up and smiled at him sheepishly, "Is that a mocha latte I smell?"

He reached for the Starbucks cup on the table next to the couch and handed it to me. "Large, hot mocha latte, skim milk, one sweetener."

I grasped the warm cup in both hands and brought it to my lips. Immediately I could smell the aroma and smiled. I leaned over and kissed him on the cheek.

"You're welcome." He wrapped me back up in his arms and we lay there in silence for awhile. I wondered if his mind was preoccupied like mine was right now.

After a long silence I decided to ask what happened that made him go home on Friday. Sometimes when I asked him about his life back home in Katy he got defensive, as if that part of his life was for him only, not for the two of us.

"So you never said why you went home Friday. Is everything okay with your mom?" I asked this knowing that he had already said that a "friend" had an emergency and needed help.

Dylan's reply came with no hesitation, "Mom is fine, at least I assume she's okay. I didn't get a chance to see her before I came back." He got up from the couch with his coffee and headed into the kitchen. I knew he was warming his coffee up, since he liked his coffee so hot that it almost scalded his tongue when he drank it.

"Oh, well I'm glad to hear everything is fine with her. So who had the big emergency then that you had to go help with?" Now I was feeling as though he was avoiding the question, as he walked out of the room without expanding on what was going on back home.

When he entered the room again from the kitchen, he reached for the remote and turned on the TV. Why was he avoiding my question?

"Dylan, what's going on?" I could tell something was bothering him and he was dodging my questions.

"Nothing. Do you want to find a movie or something?"

"So, you're not going to tell me why you were home and what you were doing all weekend?" I knew that I sounded, and felt inside, like a complete hypocrite quizzing him as if he was on trial. Perhaps it was my own guilty conscience coming out and projecting my infidelity on him.

"It was no big deal really. Marvin, a guy I graduated with, was moving back from college at SMU this weekend and he needed a hand."

That sounded perfectly reasonable, but why had he made it sound like some sort of emergency that he had to rush home for at the last minute? Honestly, I felt like there was much more to this than what he was telling me, but I wasn't going to push the issue with him. The last thing I needed was for him to start turning the conversation around on me and put me in a position to have to start lying about my weekend. Dylan never asked a lot of questions when I was out of town with "the girls" or when I made up other scenarios so I could sneak away with Kyle. Now that it was over with Kyle, I wanted to make sure that Dylan would never find out.

So I conceded. "Well, that was good that you were able to help out. Too bad you didn't get a chance to see your mom while you were in town."

He settled back in behind me on the couch with his arms around me. "Like I said, it was just a quick trip home to help out and old buddy from high school, have a few beers when we were all done, and then right back Sunday morning." He seemed relieved that I had dropped the line of questioning. "Let's do something fun today, just the two of us."

This was definitely not Dylan. Dylan was outgoing and fun, but never spontaneous and romantic. Was he overcompensating for something?

Again, I decided to just roll with it and not read too much into it. I wonder if he ever noticed a change in me after I had come back from a trip with Kyle? Had I overdone it with gestures and nervous conversation trying to hide my guilt and infidelity?

"I'd love that," I smiled and leaned in to kiss him on the cheek. "And I love you."

In that moment, I knew I had made a horrible mistake with Kyle. Dylan was the man I loved, and it was time to start focusing on moving forward with him...slowly.

Lindsey

I had always pictured my senior year making memories with my classmates, and of course with Michael. Never in my wildest dreams would I have imagined stepping into the halls of that school on the last first day of my high school years without Michael by my side.

The entire community had been affected by Michael's death. He was an amazing athlete and student, and a great friend to everyone that knew him. His memorial service was overwhelming, with the church spilling over with friends, family, community members, and classmates all wanting to pay their respects and mourn this tremendous loss. His football coach gave the eulogy and Mac struggled through a letter he had written to Michael. Keri, Trisha, Chris, Mac, and I all huddled together in the third pew of the church, arms linked holding each other together as if that would keep us from crumbling.

At the graveside burial, we all laid white roses on his casket to symbolize our friendship. Along with a white rose, I placed a homecoming boutonniere adorned with ribbons displaying his football number "23" on one ribbon and on the other was a heart next to our initials. It was the same one I had given him at homecoming the previous year. Despite what had happened between us, I loved Michael. I had loved him for so long that I didn't know how to not love him.

It was easier for me to forgive him for the things he had done, than to forgive myself. After the events that transpired at the beach house, I had no reason to feel guilty about being with Dylan, and if things had turned out differently I may not have felt that way. But in my mind, Michael's death was my fault. I blamed myself. Maybe if he hadn't been angry and hurt then he wouldn't have been distracted. If he wasn't distracted, maybe he would've seen the car pulling out and been able to avoid the impact.

Maybe. What if. Could've. Would've. Should've.

All things that would haunt me for years to come.

I retreated to my room after getting home from the burial and barely emerged over the next three days only to occasionally eat and shower. My friends all kept texting, but I just ignored their messages. Several had stopped by, but I never answered the door.

I wanted to be alone to grieve. I needed time to wrap my head around a life without Michael in it. Nothing anyone could say would bring him back and erase the pain that was ripping at my insides.

Finally, after a few days of exile, there was a knock on my bedroom door which I ignored as I had for several days.

"Linds? Linds, can I come in?"

It was Mac. There was no doubt that he was suffering as deeply as I was right now. Still, how could I help him with his grief when I couldn't even get a handle on my own?

"Mac, I just want to be alone."

"I know, I feel the same way. No one seems to know what to say, and I just want everyone to stop asking me what I need and if I'm okay. I'm not okay." I could hear in his voice that he was breaking down, and my heart ached for him. Mac and I were like siblings we were so close, and I knew that losing Michael was crushing him.

My pain and agony would have to wait. He needed me. He needed someone who could sit in the silence with him and not need words, just the presence of someone near.

My legs felt heavy and bogged down, but I swung my feet to the floor next to my bed, pulled on a sweatshirt and made my way slowly to the door.

When I unlocked the handle and opened the door, there he was, slumped on the floor next to the door, head in his hands and tears streaming down his cheeks. I touched his shoulder and felt his body start to shake as he let go of the tears.

I lowered myself to the floor and nudged myself in between his arms and wrapped him up in mine. Selfishly, I had been so consumed by my own grief that I couldn't see that others around me were hurting and needed support.

Mac was like a brother to me and I had shut him out. It was time for me to lean on others and be leaned upon.

"Mac, I'm so sorry for not being there for you. We're going to get through this together, I promise." I hugged him tight and accepted his embrace.

We spent the afternoon sitting outside in the sunshine next to the pool just relaxing and enjoying the warm of the sun's rays and the quiet of the day. I floated on a raft in the pool, while Mac lay on the edge of the deck with his feet floating in the water.

"Hey Linds, I was thinking of not playing football this fall."

I couldn't believe what I was hearing. Football meant everything to Mac, Chris, and Michael. Mac was planning on going to Baylor on a football scholarship after graduation, the exact plan his brother had before he was killed.

"Mac, why would you do that? Just because Michael is gone doesn't mean you need to stop living your life." I couldn't decide whether I was saying this for him, or for myself. In the past few days I was contemplating my future as well. Of course, I had already decided before any of the recent events, that I wasn't leaving the Houston area like my friends.

"It's not going to be the same without him this year. Coach is already replacing him with a sophomore and I just can't step on that field without him."

The three of them had played together since they were in grade school. Summer leagues, football camps…they lived and breathed football. But for Mac it was even harder because of losing his brother who was a football god in our community and every other player's hero.

"Michael would want you to play. In fact, he would be pissed if you quit." I thought about Michael and how he always pushed others around him to keep going and work harder. He was inspiring and ambitious. His presence was intoxicating and everyone around him could feel it.

Not everyone knew the side of him that I did, and I was actually thankful that they didn't. There was so much good in him, that I was glad that he would always be remembered that way.

I slipped off my raft into the water and swam for a few minutes. The cool, crisp water refreshed my warm tanned skin. I came up from under the water and made my way to the side of the pool where he was sitting.

"I don't know, Linds. It just doesn't feel right."

"You've got to give it some time. It's only been a few days. I've tried imagining myself cheering on the sidelines without him on the field, and walking down the hallways of the school without seeing him standing at my locker waiting for me." Again, the tears came easily. "I can't picture homecoming, the Christmas ball, the senior trip, prom…any of it. It all breaks my heart, but there's nothing I can do to change it. He's gone. But we are still here and we have to keep going."

He grabbed my hand and squeezed it. "I'll do it for Michael, and for you."

I looked up at him and smiled. He had always been there for me, not because he was my boyfriend's best friend, but because he was truly my friend. I knew we would have to lean on each other these next few months to survive.

I wanted to tell him the truth about what happened that day before the accident. Blaming myself was killing me inside and other than Dylan, no one knew about that afternoon.

"There's something I need to tell you about that day. I wanted to tell you before, but I didn't know how you would react." I lifted myself out of the side of the pool and sat on the edge next to him. I was afraid to look at him, scared of seeing the disappointment in his eyes.

"What is it? You can tell me anything."

Hesitantly, I began to tell him the story. I told him all of it, starting with the party at Chad's and running into Dylan outside and almost fainting. He listened while I recounted the events that took place when Dylan came back to my house and how I slept on the couch and he slept in the chair. Scared to tell him the rest, I paused.

He again reached for my hand, "Linds, it's okay, you can tell me."

I couldn't look at him. I was ashamed and the overwhelming feeling of guilt and responsibility was suffocating me.

Mac squeezed my hand, and then reached his hand up to touch my chin. Gently, knowing that a man's hand on me may be a sensitive issue after the incident with Michael, he lifted my head toward him. "Look at me, please." Our eyes met. "You never have to be afraid to tell me anything. Michael was my friend, best friend, but you are one of the most special people in my life too. You're my best friend."

"It was my fault," I softly replied, my eyes welling again with tears.

"The accident was not your fault. It was an accident."

"You don't understand. Michael left my house angry and hurt that day, because of me. And Dylan." I looked away again. "I slept with Dylan. When Michael showed up that day to talk to me Dylan was still here. They had words briefly and then I went outside to talk to Michael. He put two and two together and realized that Dylan was there, with me, not just as a friend.

"Once he realized what was going on, he was angry. He grabbed my arm, not like the night before, but still it was enough for Dylan to come out and tell him to leave. Michael left," I paused, trying to get the rest out, "and that was the last time I saw him."

Mac was silent for what seemed like an eternity. I could only imagine what he was thinking of me now, and whether or not he would forgive me for hurting Michael.

"I'm glad Dylan was here for you that night. What Michael did to you was unforgivable."

I couldn't believe what he was saying. "But I cheated on him. How can you say what he did was unforgivable when I did the same thing to him?"

"Lindsey, I wasn't talking about that. He put his hands on you. No man should ever put his hands on a woman like that, ever. Besides, you didn't cheat on him with Dylan. After what Michael did to you that night you had every right to walk away from him and not look back."

A wave of relief came over me and I felt myself exhale for the first time since the call came about the accident. Suddenly I realized that Mac didn't seem surprised at all when I told him about Dylan.

"Did you know about Dylan? I mean, you don't seem shocked about any of this. And at the hospital, you didn't seem surprised to see him there."

"Michael told me that he found Dylan here when he came to apologize to you about what happened at the beach house. He called me when he left your house that day. I knew he was pissed and I urged him to cool off and chill for awhile before he headed back to the beach. When we hung up the phone I didn't hear from him for a few hours. He texted me and said he had gotten something to eat, and I didn't realize at the time he was with Leslie. His text said he was on his way back to the beach and would be there around 9 P.M." then he paused, "and that was the last time I heard from him."

"Why didn't you tell me that you knew about all of this, Mac?"

"Because it doesn't matter now. None of it changes anything. Michael is gone. Nothing that happened that day had anything to do with the accident that killed him. And nothing you did caused any of it either, so you have to stop feeling guilty, Linds."

"I don't know what to say." I looked at him and smiled. "Thank you. For being my friend, and for understanding."

He put his arm around me and squeezed tight.

"I'll always be here for you."

In the years to come, he would be true to his word. Mac was always by my side when I needed him. I trusted him with my life. He was the keeper of my secrets, the rock when I needed strength, and a shoulder to cry on when I needed a soft place to land.

We started our senior year a few weeks later, and with Mac and the others by my side, we stood in the rotunda in the center of the school at the first period bell where there was a makeshift memorial to Michael. Tears were shed, and many would fall in the weeks and months that followed. But we kept going.

Mac played football while I cheered on the sidelines always aware of the void where Michael was missing. The days came and went, and eventually it was homecoming weekend—the first big milestone of our senior year and the weekend that I knew would hurt beyond belief.

No one had asked me to the homecoming dance as their date, probably out of respect for Michael. Had he been there, Michael and I would no doubt have been king and queen this year, as we were prince and princess last year.

After the game, everyone dispersed to get changed and ready for the dance. I went with Keri to her house and reluctantly slipped into a dress and half-assed did my hair and makeup not caring at all what I looked like. Mac came to pick us up and I felt like a third wheel. My thoughts were mostly of Michael throughout the night as I danced and tried to put on a smile around everyone.

Twice I tried to leave early, but my friends kept me from going. As I heard my name announced as homecoming queen, I realized why they wanted me to stay so badly. Tearfully, I walked onto the stage to be crowned, wishing Michael was by my side. Mac was of course the obvious choice for king, and as he ascended the stage, I smiled, knowing that Michael would be happy looking down on us right now.

Once the dance ended, we all headed to Chad's for the after party. It was the first time I had been to a party since the night Dylan showed up here looking for me. My mind was swirling with thoughts of Michael and Dylan the entire time.

"Are you okay, Linds?" Keri sat down next behind me on the stairs. "Do you want us to take you home?"

"I'm good. Just taking it all in, I guess."

She leaned down and hugged me. "I love you, Linds, and I promise it's going to get easier."

I reached my hands up to touch her arms. "I know, and I'm so grateful for your friendship." I turned to face her, "There's something I need to ask you."

"You know you can always ask me anything."

"Well, your parents approached me a few months ago about my plans for college. There's no way I can afford to go to A&M, and after everything that's happened, I don't think I could bring myself to go anyway. Your mom and dad have offered to let me stay with them after you go away so that I can go to U of H. But if you aren't okay with it then I won't."

"Oh my god! I love it!" She threw her arms around my neck almost choking me with her hug. "Of course I'm okay with it! You practically live with me anyway."

"Thank you Keri. I don't know what I would do without you and your family. Y'all have been there for me so much through all this shit with my family, and now with Michael's death. Without you and Mac, I don't know how I'd be getting through this year so far."

Keri looked away for a minute, and I could tell that something was bothering her. "Hey, where did you go just now?" I asked.

She smiled and turned to me, "Am I really that obvious?"

"Only to me. You and I share one brain most of the time." I laughed, and put my arm around her shoulders. "You can tell me anything, you know that."

"It's Mac. I just feel like we are growing apart this year. I don't know if it's because of Michael's death or just that we're becoming different people with our own lives."

I knew how she was feeling in a way, since that's where Michael and I were last summer. "I think it's probably natural for that to happen, don't you? I mean, between what he's been through in the past few years losing his brother and then his best friend, it doesn't surprise me that he's different."

She was starting to tear up and I didn't want her to fall apart here in front of all these people.

"Ker, let's spend the day together tomorrow, just you and me, and we will talk this all out."

"Thanks, Linds. What am I going to do next year away at school while you're here? Who is going to be my person?"

"I'm always going to be your person, no matter where we go or what path we both take."

We were wiping happy tears from our eyes when Mac walked up to us. "Geez girls, this is supposed to be a party…no crying!"

We laughed and both hugged him as he scooped us up, one under each arm.

I spent another hour mingling with friends before I decided to head home. I said goodbye to Keri and Mac and promised to text when I got home. It was a gorgeous night, full of stars in the sky, so I decided just to walk the two blocks home instead of having someone drive me.

My thoughts immediately turned to Dylan. I almost expected to see him standing outside when I left as he had been twice before. As I walked, I thought of how he had come here for me that night just to make sure I was safe.

When I reached my house I sat down on the front porch and stared up at the stars for awhile. I made a wish and smiled knowing that Michael was looking down on me right now thinking that it was silly for me to still be wishing on stars.

As I looked up at the moon, I wondered where Dylan was right now and if he was looking at the same moon. Did he remember the night we sat and talked about wishing on stars? Had he forgotten about me and stayed with Melissa? It was my fault if he did. I was the one who broke the lines of communication.

He reached out to me when he got back to school after Michael's death and told me when I was ready he would be there. I just wasn't ready, and I didn't know how long it would take before I would be, if ever.

The guilt was starting to subside, but I missed Michael. Part of me was mourning his death still and the other part of me was trying to forgive him for what he had done to me. The cheating was bad enough and had caused me to question whether or not I could ever trust anyone again. But the night on the beach was the thing that really scared me the most. How could someone who claimed to love me put his hands on me like that? I knew that if I ever wanted to move past all of this, I would have to find a way to forgive him.

Dylan

I knew that Lindsey was about to graduate, but only because of Rachel. I never asked about her or brought up her name in conversation. Rachel occasionally talked to me about what was going on with her family, especially the current divorce that her mother and stepfather were in the middle of now.

I worried about Lindsey and how she was coping with everything she was being dealt right now. Her life was going through so many changes with her family issues, Michael's death, and now about to graduate and figure out what to do with her future. Just trying to handle the magnitude of death and divorce would be too much for most people. I knew she had good friends to lean on, but I still worried about her.

Several times I considered reaching out to her, but I didn't. The last time we had contact I told her that if she needed me I was here if she needed me, but I never heard from her again.

I put all my efforts into making things work with Melissa and throwing myself into our relationship to try and forget about Lindsey. I was fooling myself into believing that I could forget about what happened with her that weekend because no matter how hard I tried I just couldn't let go of her.

As the months went by, I made a conscious effort to move past the thought of ever having a future with Lindsey, and I focused on my future with Melissa. She was now working full-time at the Baylor Scott & White Medical Center in College Station, and I was finishing up my junior year of classes already since I had doubled up on credits the past two semesters. The extra course load helped me focus and stop living in the past.

I decided that summer would be the perfect time to finally take that step forward with Melissa and begin living together. So, we searched for a townhouse and after a few weeks we were signing a one-year lease on a two bedroom with all the amenities.

The night we moved in, we celebrated with a bottle of champagne and take-out Mexican food, eating on lawn chairs in the living room since our furniture wouldn't be delivered for a few more days.

I raised my glass and made a toast. "Here's to our new life together!"

She smiled, "Cheers! I can't believe we finally did it!"

I knew she had waited a long time for me to make this move, and not many other women would've been so patient. She deserved better than me.

"I'm sorry it took so long for us, actually me, to get here."

"Dylan, it wasn't just you that needed time. I thought I was ready last year, but I'm actually thankful we waited longer. I think this past year has been good for us to both become a little more stable with our lives before we could move to this point together." She set down her glass, took my hands, and said, "I love you. This is exactly where I want to be."

It was in that moment that I finally knew I had made the right decision to stay with Melissa. I wanted to be honest with her about what happened with Lindsey, but I was afraid of losing her, so I chose to stay silent.

Lindsey

Things began to change so quickly as we approached graduation in May. Keri and Mac had broken up a few months ago, and she had already started seeing someone else from Cinco Ranch. We were months from graduating, our group was diminishing quickly, and everyone had already gone their separate ways.

With senior prom looming, I had all but decided I wasn't going. I spent my entire school year focusing on my grades, getting my application in at University of Houston, working part-time, and cheering, so there wasn't much time for a social life. Not to mention, I wasn't ready for a social life especially if it entailed dating someone.

I knew Keri and her boyfriend would be going to prom at his school, so there was really no reason for me to go to ours. The week of prom, I helped her accessorize her dress and decide how to wear her hair that night.

"Linds, I can't believe we aren't going to be at prom together our senior year. So much has changed this year, it just doesn't seem real."

"I know," I sighed and lowered my head, visibly sad. "This is not at all how I imagined this year would be. I pictured you and Mac, me and Michael all at prom together, graduating, and spending the summer together before we all went to school in the fall."

I tried hiding the tears, but I could never hide my feelings from her. We were sisters, without the blood relation.

"Lindsey, is it Michael? You still miss him don't you?"

145

"Of course I do. But it's not just that, it's everything. Nothing is the way I imagined it would be. My parents, my friends, me. Everything has changed."

I had never told her about the night with Dylan. Mac knew because Michael had told him, but he swore to never say anything to anyone. When she and Mac came to the hospital the night Michael was killed, she never asked why Dylan was with me, and I never brought him up to her again. As much as I felt for Dylan, mostly I felt guilt over what had happened that day with him. Not a day went by that I didn't think about him, but I knew he was better off living his life without me complicating it.

"Is Mac going to prom with anyone?"

"No," I said, "as far as I know he's not going."

"Lindsey, why don't you and Mac go together."

I laughed, "Oh come on, be serious!"

"No, really, I'm being serious! Y'all have been friends since you were kids, and there's no reason the two of you shouldn't go together."

"I can think of several reasons. Michael. You. Do I need more?"

"Linds, Michael is gone. And I've moved on with Justin. Mac will always be special to me, but he and I are over. Why can't you two just go as friends?"

Actually, she had a point. Mac was one of my best friends, even now that he and Keri weren't dating anymore. We had spent even more time together actually in the past few months than we ever had before.

"Keri, don't you think that would be weird if we went together? The last thing I would want to do is to do something that would upset you."

"I'm the one that suggested it. Do it. Call him, now." She handed me my cell phone and had already hit send to dial his number.

"Keri!" I yelled. Then he was on the other end of the phone and I was caught off guard.

"Hello? Linds? What's up?" I was silent. "Lindsey, hello?"

"Hi Mac." I was nervous for some reason. This was Mac, one of my best friends. There was no need to be nervous. "Whatcha doin?"

He laughed, "Not much, you?"

"Oh, just hanging out."

"Is something wrong, Linds? You sound strange."

"Well, um, I was wondering if you had decided whether or not you were going to prom on Saturday?" Oh shit, no turning back now.

146

"I hadn't planned on it. Now that Keri and I aren't together, I just figured there was no reason to go."

"Oh, yeah, well that makes sense." I was fumbling with my words and my palms were starting to sweat. Why was I feeling like this?

"What about you? Are you going?"

"Well, I wasn't going to, but I don't know, maybe." Would he pick up on what was happening or would I have to spell this out for him and just come right out and ask?

He seemed surprised at my answer, "Oh, wow, did someone ask you?"

"No!" I quickly replied, realizing that he clearly wasn't getting the hint. Keri was looking at me and urging me to just ask him. This felt so foreign to me right now. "No, I just was thinking that maybe I should, I mean we should since it's our senior prom."

There, I put it out there for him.

"Yeah, you should definitely go."

Crap, he didn't get it.

I looked at Keri and threw my hands up in the air. "You know what, I will. I'm going to prom." There was a silence on the phone. I didn't know what more to say. "Okay, so I'll let you go."

"Wait, Linds! So if you're going, then maybe I should go too." I smiled, he got it. "I don't want you to be there by yourself."

"Okay, yeah, that's great, thanks!" He still hadn't said anything about going together, but at least he would be there.

"Actually, why don't we go together? I mean, as friends of course."

I smiled, unsure of why this made me so happy, but it did.

"I'd like that." I paused for a moment. "I guess I better find a dress." Oddly, I could almost feel him smiling through the phone. I didn't understand what I was feeling right now, but I knew that it was the happiest I had felt in a very long time.

"Great, um yeah, so let me know when you find a dress so I can match up my tie." He sounded nervous. "Should we go to dinner first?"

"Yeah, that would be great! Just something simple, you know, as friends." I could feel the warmth in my face and Keri was smiling at me from ear to ear.

"Ok great, I'll figure something out and let you know."

"Well, I guess I'll get working on a dress."

"Hey, Linds, thank you. For saying yes. I'm really looking forward to it."

My heart felt different than it had in awhile, and I could feel myself blushing. "Me too."

I hung up the phone and was silent, unsure of what to say to Keri. I had just been asked to our senior prom by Mac, who up until a few months ago, had been her "first love".

She broke the silence by grabbing my hands in hers. "Lindsey, this is a good thing. Don't you see what I see?"

"I don't know what you're talking about."

"You and Mac have a bond that no one else can understand, and that's something you should be thankful to have. He's a wonderful guy, and he adores you. He always has."

"Keri, Mac has always been my friend. I've never thought of him in any other way before."

"Well, maybe you should start." She smiled at me and squeezed my hands, "Let's go! We need to find you a dress!"

When prom day came, I was unexpectedly nervous and worried about whether having Mac as my actual date would be awkward. We had been friends, almost like brother and sister, nearly our entire lives. I had never looked at him as anything other than my friend, my boyfriend's best friend, and for some reason that was starting to change.

Mac was tall, muscular, and athletic with a wide smile and bright cornflower blue eyes. His hair was slightly wavy, dark chestnut brown, and he had huge dimples when he smiled. All of these things went unnoticed to me for all of these years, until now.

At the salon, Keri and I both had our hair done in updos, mine a sleek low bun at the nape of my neck, understated and classic. We parted at the salon as she was going to finish getting ready with a friend that went to school with her new boyfriend since they were all going together.

Back at my house, I finished my make-up and painted my nails to compliment my dress. The dress was long and fitted with an open back and side slit to my mid thigh, deep midnight blue edged with rhinestones. I purchased heels, which I rarely wore, so that at 6'2" Mac wouldn't tower over me.

I had ordered a boutonnière for him and was now pacing the floor waiting for my date to arrive.

The doorbell rang at 4:58 P.M. to begin our evening. When I opened the door, it was as if I was seeing him for the very first time. He was dressed in a dark grey double breasted suit with a navy blue tie, his hair neatly groomed and his blue eyes seemed to sparkle as he smiled at me.

"Wow, Lindsey, you look…um, you're beautiful." He was smiling and staring at me with wide eyes.

I could feel my cheeks heating up and no doubt turning red blushing at hearing those words. Beautiful…I don't think I had ever heard those words directed toward me until that moment.

"And you clean up pretty well too." I felt myself flirting with him, and it felt natural and right.

"Thank you." He stood holding a small clear box containing a corsage of mini, fuchsia-tone pink roses, silver ribbons, and white baby's breath. "This is for you." He outstretched his hands holding the small box.

"Can you put it on me? I also have something for you." I opened the door wider and stepped aside, "Why don't you come in for a minute and we can exchange them?"

He stepped into my house and I had to catch my breath as he ascended the front step past me and into the foyer.

I took his boutonnière from the box and pinned it on the lapel of his suit coat. He placed my corsage around my wrist and gently held my hand.

"It's gorgeous, Mac, thank you. I love pink roses."

"I'm glad you like it. The woman at the florist said that dark pink roses symbolize appreciation and gratitude." He was starting to blush a little as he spoke. "You've always been there for me, ever since I've know you, and been a great friend to me."

I was taken aback by this. "You actually went to the florist and picked this out yourself?"

"Um, yes. Does that surprise you?"

"Well, actually it does." I was feeling a little overwhelmed at this gesture and his sincerity behind it. "It means a lot to me that you put so much thought into picking out the perfect flowers." I was starting to feel the tears building and I was afraid of turning this moment into something sad, when it was truly a happy moment. I looked up at him. "Mac, thank you. For making me feel the happiest I have felt in a very long time."

He took my hands, "And the night hasn't even started yet."

As we left my house and walked to his car, he held my hand and I let him lead. Like a true southern gentleman, he opened my car door for me and closed it once I was inside. He took me to a fantastic little Italian restaurant where we enjoyed a great dinner and even better conversation. Talking to Mac was always easy, never uncomfortable silence.

We found ourselves lingering over a shared piece of tiramisu for dessert and suddenly realized we were late for the dance. He paid the bill and once again, led me to the car opening all doors for me along the way. I tried not to compare him to Michael, but it was refreshing to have someone doing all of the right things with no effort.

When we reached the dance, we walked arm and arm into the ballroom, both beaming with happiness. We found Trisha and Chris on the dance floor and joined them. A few fast songs later, the disc jockey transitioned to a slow song and couples paired up all around us.

We awkwardly lingered for a moment, then as I started to turn away from the dance floor, I felt his gently touch on my arm.

His hand was outstretched. "Lindsey, would you like to dance?"

I smiled and took his hand. "I'd love to."

He led me by my hand onto the dance floor, and took me into his arms, pulling me close to him. My head rested in the center of his chest and although the music rang in my ears, all I could hear was his heartbeat. I inhaled the scent of his cologne and in that moment I felt something I had never felt with Michael, or Dylan. I felt safe. I felt as though we were the only two people in the room. Right then, my heart was happy.

We spent the rest of the night dancing with our friends, and when it came time for the crowning of the prom king and queen, we ascended the stage as our names were announced. Last year, Michael and I were the prince and princess of the prom as juniors, and if he were here now, there was no doubt that he would've been on that stage with me. I hoped that Mac didn't feel as though he was a second place to Michael. Michael was gone, and life was continuing on as it should.

We took the floor for our dance with the prom court. He held me tight and whispered in my ear, "Are you having a good time?"

I lifted my head and peered up at him into those beautiful blue eyes. "I am. This has been such a wonderful night. Thank you." I reached up and kissed him on the cheek.

I saw his cheeks flush and he smiled down at me. "I'm glad. So am I." He kissed me on the forehead and we continued dancing.

When the song was over we stood still for a moment, just taking the moment in a little longer. He pulled me closer and held me just a little tighter.

"Linds, I have a surprise for you." We broke from our embrace and he smiled at me, "Do you mind if we leave a little early? There's something I want to show you."

I looked up at him and grinned at him, "What are you up to, Mac?"

"Do you trust me?" he asked.

"Of course. More than anyone."

He leaned in and whispered in my ear, grazing my cheek with his lips, "Then take my hand and let's go."

In the car, I kept trying to get him to tell me where we were going, but he refused to give me any hints. I loved surprises. There weren't enough good, happy surprises in my life lately.

We drove for about twenty minutes until he pulled into the parking lot of the country club in the subdivision we lived in.

"What are we doing here?"

He was holding my hand the entire ride, and he raised it to his lips and kissed it gently. "Stop asking questions and just trust me." He exited the car and came around to my side to open the door for me then help me out. He had opened the trunk from inside before he got out and as we walked around the back of the vehicle, he reached into the trunk and took out a small cooler, a blanket, and some type of bag.

I looked at him sideways and jokingly laughed, "If you pull out a shovel next I'm going to start running."

"Ha ha! Stop! You said you trusted me, so trust me." He closed the trunk and we started walking toward the country club building.

We reached the carport where they stored the golf carts and he set down his bag and fished a key out of the pocket of his sport coat. He set the blanket, cooler, and bag in the basket of the cart and grabbed my hand.

"Your chariot awaits."

I laughed, "What are you up to?" I knew he worked summers here on the golf course so I didn't surprise me that he had a key to the carts.

He was really enjoying this. "You'll see."

I climbed into the passenger seat of the cart and he walked around to get in the driver's side. As we drove, the night air was becoming chilly and my arms were covered in goosebumps.

"Linds, are you cold?"

"A little, I guess." I didn't want him to feel bad, since obviously he had put some thought into this surprise.

He slowed the cart and took off his coat, draping it around my shoulders. "Better?"

"Perfect." I looked at him and smiled. How was I just now finally seeing him like this for the first time?

After a couple minutes, he stopped and we parked next to the green on one of the golf holes.

He got out of the cart and turned to me. "Stay right here for one minute. And close your eyes. No peeking."

I couldn't help but smile at him as he made his way around to the back of the cart and unloaded the items he had taken from the trunk of the car. I closed my eyes and thought about what an amazing night we'd had so far.

After a minute or two, he was again at my side.

"Ok, take my hand." He grabbed my hands and led me off of the cart.

I was giggling, "Mac, what is going on?"

"You'll see, just a little bit further." He was leading me blindly across the grass.

"Oh!" I shouted, "My shoes!" My heels were now sinking into the soft grass below.

"I'm sorry, I never thought about that. Here, put your arms around my neck." He scooped me up in his arms and I held on tightly, still laughing.

I reached down and pulled my heels off and dangled them from my hands behind his back. Then, he set me down and I could feel the softness of the flannel blanket under my bare feet.

"Ok," he said, "open your eyes."

As I opened my eyes and tried to regain my focus, I couldn't believe what I was seeing in front of me.

I turned to look at him. "You did all this for me?" Stretched out in front of us was a flannel blanket with several lit candles next to it, chocolate covered strawberries, and a bottle of sparking cider and two champagne flutes. Laying on the blanket was a small telescope. I was in awe. "Mac, what is all of this?"

He seemed nervous, "I wanted this to be perfect for you tonight. I knew this isn't how you expected your prom night to be this year, going with me instead of Michael. So I just wanted to make it special for you. For us."

It took me a minute to find the words I wanted. "Mac, this isn't at all how I thought this night would be." He looked away, and I reached slowly for his face. I touched his face with my hands and brought our eyes to meet. "It's more than I ever could've dreamed it would be."

He looked down at me and smiled, relieved. And in that moment, we shared our first kiss.

We sat down and toasted our non-alcoholic sparkling drinks and ate strawberries. I asked how he knew that they were my favorite, and he said Keri had told him. Who would've thought that she would be the one to help orchestrate this evening? I knew she had also helped Michael plan the night we lost our virginity together. And now here she was helping Mac plan this. Clearly she saw something that the two of us had been missing.

I glanced over remembering the telescope. "What's that for?" I asked.

"Well, that night at the beach before, well…before things got bad… you had gone out to the fire before the rest of us. I saw you from the back deck of the beach house. You were looking up at the stars. Michael came out onto the deck and laughed when he saw you. I asked him why he was laughing and he said that you were always wishing on stars." He paused, lost in his memory. "And I guess I just kinda remembered that. So I thought this would be a good place to see the stars. Maybe even make a wish on one."

I stared at him for a moment. He had put so much thought into this and I was in complete awe of him right now.

"I don't know what to say." I felt myself starting to get emotional and my face was feeling flush and tingly. Memories of Michael and me, Keri and Mac, all of us together were starting to flood back into my mind. I turned to him as I felt a tear run down my cheek. "Mac, how did we get here? Michael is gone, Keri has moved on, and now there's just you and me."

He smiled and wiped the tear from my face. "I miss Michael every day, and when Keri and I first broke up I missed her too. Michael's death changed everything, for all of us. But I believe that things happen for a reason, and we end up exactly where we are meant to be. I have no explanation for what happened to Michael, but we have to move on with life."

"I miss him too," I said, "but I'm ready to let go. I have so much guilt still from that weekend, and I'm still trying to forgive myself."

He pulled me close to him, my back against his chest, and wrapped me up in his arms. "Lindsey, I know this is still really fresh for both of us, so we don't have to rush anything. But, I'm feeling something with you that I don't think I've ever felt before. And I really want to see where it goes."

I smiled and snuggled into him closer, "I feel it too. This night has been amazing."

He kissed my cheek, "It's just starting, Linds."

We sat for awhile just enjoying the quiet of the night, the sky lit by the moon and a million stars. He set up the mini telescope and showed me some of the constellations that he knew. I was impressed by his knowledge and by this elaborate evening he had planned for us.

It was nearing 1 A.M. and we packed up our things and headed back to the country club. As we walked to his car after parking the golf cart, my hand felt so natural inside the pocket of his. We reached his car and he dropped the picnic items into the truck and opened the door helping me in once again.

The drive to my house seemed way too short, as I was wishing we had more time. He pulled into the driveway at my house and we shared a few more soft, yet passionate kisses in the driveway before he got out and came around to let me out.

Once we were at my doorstep I turned to him. "Mac, this has been perfect. Thank you. I never could've dreamed it would be like this." I wrapped my arms around him and the feel of his arms around me was the best I had felt in a very long time.

He took my face gently in his hands. "You don't have to thank me. I enjoyed every single minute of it."

We kissed again, and the feel of his body pressing against mine sent electricity through me. But I knew I wasn't ready for anything more than this right now. Mac drew slightly back from me and then kissed me on the forehead.

"Goodnight, Lindsey."

I smiled. There was no pressure for anything more than this right now. Mac knew me as well as anyone, maybe better.

"Goodnight, Mac. Text me when you get home so I know you're there safe."

"Of course." He kissed me again and then left.

For a moment, I stood there watching him drive off thinking to myself how lucky I was at this very moment. Did I deserve to be happy again? Had I really ever been happy? All those years I thought Michael and I were happy, I was just fooling myself. In the beginning things were good, but Michael was self-centered and cared more about himself than he ever did me. But I loved him anyway. It was time to let go of him, and let myself be happy.

Melissa

The first few months living with Dylan were amazing, and I was so thankful that I had made the decision to end things with Kyle to stay with him. We were having fun playing house, decorating our new home together, cooking dinner on date night, and sharing our lives together finally.

It took a few months after ending things with Kyle to feel like myself again, and really start to focus on moving forward with Dylan. Whatever happened when he had gone home that weekend to "help a friend" had changed him. I knew that there was more to the story than what he had told me, but I never pried further into it with him. I had my own indiscretions to overcome, so I'd be a hypocrite to fault him for anything he had done.

I told myself when I started to feel the guilt creep back up that everyone makes mistakes and I should forgive myself for what I had done. The important thing was that I had ended things with Kyle and there had been no more contact with him at all since the day we said goodbye at the airport.

Dylan and I were having a quiet night in tonight, so I picked up something for dinner and headed home from work to settle in for the night. He texted around five to say he was on his way and would be home soon.

He walked in the door twenty minutes later with a bouquet of flowers and a huge smile on his face.

Lately he had started these little surprises for me and I couldn't have been happier. This was the man I had wanted all along. I guess sometimes we need to take the long way around to eventually get to where we need to be. Both of us had, and thankfully we ended up here.

"Dylan, they're beautiful! I don't know what I did to deserve them, but let me know and I'll keep doing it." I rushed into his arms and kissed him deeply, feeling his light afternoon stubble brush against my lips.

"Well, if that's the reaction I'm going to get from you, then I'll be doing this more often." He grinned at me with that sexy smile of his and tucked his free arm up under my back and pulled me into him. "I love you Liss." He kissed me again and I felt the charge through my body that I always got when he pressed himself into me.

"I love you too." I sheepishly smiled at him with my eyes. "I haven't started dinner yet. Want an appetizer?" I kissed him again and lightly nibbled at his bottom lip, a move that always drove him crazy, signaling that I wasn't referring to food right now.

He set the flowers down on the side table by the front door, grabbed my hand in his, and led me to the bedroom.

Dylan slowly removed my clothes, piece by piece, teasing me with his fingers and his mouth as he progressed his way down my body. He knew exactly what made me feel good, and he loved making me climax. I lay down on the bed and he slid the last item of clothing off of me and pressed his lips against my body just inside my left thigh. I felt his hand run up the inside of my right leg, stopping just before he reached the top, knowing this was driving me wild. His tongue gently touched the outside as his fingers started to explore inside me, and within minutes I couldn't hold back as I came undone. He looked up at me and smiled, knowing that he had the power to make me feel like this.

His lips were on mine, as I felt him slowly and fully enter me. I felt myself catch my breath as I took him inside me and pressed my hips into him.

We made love twice that evening, once before dinner and then later taking our time and making it last into the late hours of the night. This was always the one thing that Dylan and I got right, and finally the rest was all starting to fall in place too.

I woke in the morning before he did and went to the kitchen to get coffee for us both. As I waited for the coffee, I looked around at this home that we were creating for the two of us. I was happy, finally.

"Good morning, handsome." I snuggled up next to him and set our coffees on the nightstand next to the bed. I kissed him on his chest and then up to his lips. "How did you sleep?"

"I slept like a baby. Of course, I think I could attribute that to you." He kissed my forehead and I settled into the curve of his arm.

"Maybe I'll call in sick today and we can just stay here in bed all day."

"Wouldn't that be perfect?" He stretched and reached for his shorts lying on the floor next to the bed. "I have to get to class. We're doing a review before the final tomorrow. I can't believe I'm almost done."

"We will celebrate when your finals are over. Maybe a repeat of last night." I kissed him and reached for my coffee.

"That works for me." He smiled and headed for the shower.

I was loving this place that we were in, like being in the "honeymoon phase" of a marriage. I knew that someday we would be heading down that path, and although I had been impatient in the beginning, I was learning to take things slower with Dylan now. It was okay to take our time and not rush things.

Dylan

$\mathcal{I}$ knew at some point I would ask Melissa to marry me. When months turned into almost two years, I knew that Lindsey and I would never be anything more than what we were that night. I would always have unresolved feelings for her, but that I needed to let go.

I knew that I would be happy with Melissa. We'd been living together for awhile now, and things were going great. Looking back, we probably should've done it a long time ago.

I enlisted the help of her former roommate and best friend Shelly to help with picking out a ring. Since we had moved in together, Melissa hadn't mentioned marriage, and neither had I. Hopefully that would mean that the proposal would catch her completely off guard.

"Shelly, thanks for helping me with this. I'm such a guy and totally clueless about this stuff." I could feel my palms starting to sweat already. Even though I knew this was the right move for me, I was still nervous.

"Relax, Dylan. I've got this covered for you! Melissa told me a long time ago that her dream ring was a one-carat, princess-cut solitaire, white gold and low profile setting. She didn't want something that would get caught on her gloves at work, and she wanted to be able to wear it every day."

We were having a quick lunch at a small café around the corner from the jewelry store, and I hated lying to Melissa about where I was when she texted me and asked if I could get away for a quick lunch. I told her I was going to be stuck at work all day instead of telling her the truth.

Since I had graduated in May, I had taken a job at a marketing firm and was working crazy hours trying to prove myself. I had done an internship there my final semester and they hired me full-time as soon as I was done with finals.

Over lunch I told Shelly a little about my plans for the proposal. I was thinking about taking Melissa away for the weekend, but Shelly thought that she might expect it if I did that. She thought maybe something a little more spontaneous, like a sunset at Lake Bryan or at the top of the ferris wheel at the amusement park.

Melissa loved going to the lake and watching the sunset, so that would be the perfect idea. We went quite often and shared a bottle of wine, some snacks, and sat near the shore until the sun had faded. I'd wait for the perfect evening in July when it was warm enough to stay past the sunset.

We headed into the jewelry store and I knew immediately when I saw the ring that it was the perfect one for her. I knew her size, too, because I had taken one of her rings from her jewelry collection that morning so I could get it sized correctly.

I waited very impatiently for July, hoping she wouldn't notice my anxiousness and think something was going on. Shelly was going to set everything up for me so that I could just spontaneously mention a quick trip to the lake for a sunset.

I picked up all of her favorites from the local deli—tomato mozzarella salad with balsamic glaze, crostini with guacamole and fresh pico de gallo, rolled roast beef and turkey, and potato salad. It was a hodgepodge of items but all her favorites nonetheless. I also stopped at the bakery for mini cream puffs and a large slice of tiramisu. At the liquor store, I bought a nice bottle of Chianti and a small bottle of Baileys Irish Crème for after dinner coffee drinks.

I dropped everything off at Shelly's apartment along with a large picnic basket, blanket, and a thermos with fresh coffee from Starbucks. We had decided on a secluded spot just under a bluff that would be the perfect place to enjoy the sunset and have a little privacy if there were others there as well.

The plan was for me to text Melissa and tell her that I would take care of dinner tonight. The sun would be setting sometime around 8:45 P.M. so I wanted to get her to the lake by 7:30 so we had time to eat, relax, and I was definitely going to need a drink to calm my nerves. I wasn't nervous about getting engaged or whether she would say yes or not, but I was worried about pulling it all together without her suspecting anything.

Back at home I waited impatiently for her to arrive, and my anxiety was increasing with each moment that passed. I heard her car pull into the driveway just a few minutes after seven, so I went into the kitchen to wait and begin the plan for the evening.

I stood with my back to the door and my head in the refrigerator as if I was trying to decide what to make for dinner.

"Hey, babe," she greeted me once she was in the door, "whatcha doin?"

"Trying to figure out what to do for dinner." I would have to put on my best poker face if I was going to pull this off.

"I thought you said you would handle dinner tonight?" She seemed slightly irritated as she asked.

"Oh yeah, I've got it covered. I just haven't figured it all out yet." I was going to lead her off track. "Is there anything you're craving?"

She walked into the kitchen and gave me a quick kiss on the cheek as I still stood bent over looking into the fridge. "I don't care, babe, whatever you can come up with is fine with me. It's been a long day and I just want to change into my sweats and hit the couch."

"Well, I can't find anything in here to make for dinner. Why don't we go out to eat tonight? Chinese or Thai?" I was trying not to laugh knowing that this was going to definitely irritate her, making it seem like I had put no thought into this at all.

I could hear her sigh. "Dylan, I just wanted to come home and relax. Can we order some take-out for something? I'll even eat cereal. I just don't want to leave the house."

Okay, this was going to be more difficult than I thought.

I went over and put my arms around her to try and soften her up a little. "Oh, come on Liss, let's go grab a few beers and a pizza. Just throw on something comfy, nothing fancy, and let's go. I'll drive, and I'll treat."

She smiled, "Give me ten minutes."

Step one, get her dressed and into the truck…check.

I had come up with the idea of going to Pete's Restaurant for a pizza, antipasto, and a few beers since the lake was on the way to Pete's. We neared the exit for the road to the lake and I started to get nervous, wondering what I'd say once she started asking questions about why I was taking the exit. She must've been preoccupied because she didn't say anything until we neared the parking area for the lake.

"Wait, what are we doing here? I thought we were going to Pete's?"

I smiled, turned to her, and grabbed her hand bringing it to my lips. "I have a surprise for you."

She lit up, and I loved seeing her smile. Melissa was stunningly beautiful with dark auburn hair and bright blue eyes that sparkled when she smiled.

"You know I love surprises!" She was beaming from ear to ear.

I pulled into a parking spot and rushed to open her door for her. We were on a date, and whenever we were on a date, I pulled out all of the stops. I grabbed her hand, and she stepped out of the truck and kissed me. "Thank you."

"Don't thank me yet," I smiled. "You haven't seen your surprise yet."

I held her hand as we walked toward the lake. I knew she loved coming here, so this would be a perfect place for a proposal. We made our way out to the bluff, and I helped her down the stairs and around the corner.

"Close your eyes," I said. I held her hand and guided her as I made my way over to where Shelly had set the scene for us. "Almost there, just another few steps. Okay, open your eyes."

She was in amazement of what was in front of her. "Oh Dylan, what is all of this for?" Tears were filling her eyes, and I could tell she was completely caught off guard.

"I just wanted to plan a romantic evening for us. You've worked so hard lately, so I wanted to give you a relaxing night off."

We took a seat on the blanket, and I reached into the picnic basket and pulled out the bottle of wine and glasses, pouring us each a glass.

"How about a toast?" I raised my glass. "To our new home, and our future."

She raised her glass and brought it to mine. "I'll drink to that."

I laid out the items from the picnic basket and we took our time eating and having good conversation. She was pleased and a little surprised I think at how much thought I had put into the items I chose, knowing they were all of her favorites.

The sun was beginning to set and I knew the time was almost right for me to get to why we were really here tonight. I asked her if she wanted to walk for a few minutes since we were finished eating.

I stood up and reached for her hand to help her up. We walked holding hands down near the water to a spot that was secluded and I stopped and took her wine glass from her hand and set it down.

"What's going on? Is something wrong?" She was starting to get suspicious of my behavior.

"Everything is fine, I just want to talk for a few minutes." I smiled and brushed her hair off her face, "You're so beautiful, Melissa. I hope you know how much I love you and I appreciate how you've been patient and stuck by me these past few years. I know that I can be distant and sometimes difficult, but I'm working on being better and I'll continue to work on it too. I just want to make you happy and take care of you."

She was starting to tear up, and I lowered to one knee and pulled the ring box from my pocket. Her eyes widened and she was smiling from ear to ear knowing what was coming next.

"Melissa, please say you'll marry me and give me the chance to make you happy for the rest of your life."

I opened the ring box revealing the princess-cut solitaire I had chosen with the help of her best friend. She was crying as I took it from the box and put it on her finger.

"Yes, of course my answer is yes!" she cried.

I stood up and kissed her, then wrapped her up in my arms. The moment was perfect. The sun was setting, and she was thrilled beyond belief.

She was wiping tears from her eyes and staring at the sparkling diamond I had just placed on her ring finger. "How did you do all of this? The picnic, the ring, the sunset, it's all just perfect."

"Well, I have to admit I had a little help pulling it off."

"Shelly, right?"

"She was a godsend. I couldn't have done it without her."

"Dylan, I can't believe this is happening. You've made me so happy."

I took her hand and we walked back to the picnic spot and I poured Bailey's and coffee for us both and brought out the desserts. She again was amazed at how I had managed to pick out all of her favorites.

We stayed there until it got too cold, and we packed up and drove home an engaged couple. She was calling and texting all of her friends and family, and I knew in that moment that I had made the right decision to marry her. She loved me, and I knew we would have a happy life together.

I thought briefly of Lindsey as I started to see the stars making their appearance for the evening. I wondered if she was looking up at them right now, and if she was doing okay. From time to time I would ask Rachel how she was and hope that she was doing well. All I wanted was for her to be happy and safe.

Lindsey

Senior prom was the beginning of something amazing between me and Mac that I never in a million years saw coming. He had made every second of that night special and it was truly the best night of my life.

We finished our senior year and graduated together spending nearly every moment together. The summer following graduation was so different than the previous ones spent with our other friends coupled off with each other. Keri was spending most of her time with Justin and had decided to change her plans for college and head to Texas Christian University with him. Our other friends were all working and getting things ready to go in the fall.

Mac and I continued spending all our free time together, and I felt myself falling harder and harder for him with each day that passed. We took things slowly, not wanting to rush into anything. He knew that I still struggled some days with the guilt and sadness that I felt from losing Michael. He also knew about Dylan and about my feelings I had for him in the past. I told Mac about the crush I had on Dylan for years, and the night we kissed a few years ago. He already knew about what happened between us the weekend Michael passed away.

I expressed my insecurities to him about the fact that his long-term girlfriend was my best friend, and it was still a little awkward for me to now be filling the shoes that she once did. Keri had assured us both that she was thrilled that the two of us were now together and that it made her happy we had each other.

For the Fourth of July weekend, Mac surprised me with a trip to South Padre Island, just the two of us. His parents had a timeshare there and we were able to use it for the weekend.

167

His parents had given him a new Jeep Wrangler for graduation, so we took the soft top off to enjoy the sunshine and warm air as we drove the two hours to the beach. I was prepared that this would be the first time that Mac and I would be spending the night together in that we would be actually having sex tonight, not just sleeping in the same bed as we had been doing often lately. I loved being wrapped in his arms and breathing him in while we snuggled together. Mac was my best friend, other than Keri, and now we had taken this friendship to a whole new level.

I was nervous about being with him that night because even though we'd been dating for a few months now, I was worried that taking this final step in our relationship would change things for us. But I trusted him, and I knew that it felt right. Sex wasn't something I took lightly, and I wasn't "experienced" like a lot of girls my age. I had only been with Michael and Dylan, and I never wanted to be the kind of girl that slept around with different guys.

I knew that Mac had been with only two girls other than Keri, so he too wasn't exactly experienced. He had been so thoughtful with our prom night, and all of our other dates since then were equally special, so I knew that even if he had nothing planned we would still have a wonderful weekend.

Mac's family was borderline upper class, and they never traveled without going first-class. Their timeshare was spectacular! I couldn't believe that this was where we would be staying for the weekend.

The house was directly on the beach with a huge, wrap-around deck, outdoor kitchen and plunge pool area with fireplace. Inside was a massive gourmet kitchen, living room overlooking the water with a solid wall of glass windows and doors, and the master suite had sliding doors leading outside to the private hot tub.

Mac had bought groceries and was unloading them and putting them away while I took my bags into the master bedroom. I went into the kitchen to help and he surprised me with a bouquet of flowers—daisies which were my favorite. I beamed with delight and kissed him deeply and slowly.

"You're amazing, Mac."

He was starting to blush a little, and his dimples were showing as he smiled back at me. His deep blue eyes sparkled at me and I could feel myself fall a little further in love with him each moment we were together. He made me feel safe and loved. I knew that as long as I was with him, I would always be happy.

We spent the afternoon on the beach lying in the sun, and Mac did a little surfing while I read for awhile. As the afternoon started to fade to evening, we both showered separately and started working on dinner together. We both loved to cook and spent many evenings playing house at my mom's, since she was never home, making dinner together and trying out new recipes.

Tonight we were going to grill some homemade pizzas and make a large antipasto salad. I made a large pitcher of sweet tea with a little fresh mint that he had picked up at the store at my request. We put the salad in the fridge while we went to the deck to grill the pizzas.

"Mac, I feel like we're an old married couple." I laughed as I watched him lighting the grill as I brought our iced teas out to the deck behind him.

He turned to me, "Just a preview of life in fifty years." Mac walked over to me and wrapped his arms around me. "Linds, you make me so happy." He kissed me and I felt the warmth I always did when his lips met mine.

"Me too. I didn't know that being with someone could be like this." I looked away because I was thinking of Michael right now.

He touched my chin and turned my gaze back to meet his eyes. "Lindsey, it's okay to talk about him. We don't have to pretend that he wasn't a part of your life. He was my best friend. Sometimes I feel guilty because I'm here with you and so happy, but he's…gone."

I knew what he was feeling because I had the same kind of thoughts.

"Mac, I thought I loved him, and maybe I really did in some way. But that wasn't love. He controlled me. With you I feel like I can be myself and that's enough for you."

"You're more than enough for me. Lindsey, I love you."

I couldn't believe this was happening.

"I love you too."

We enjoyed dinner on the deck and went for a long walk on the beach until the sun went down. Back at the house we grabbed a couple blankets and went out onto the deck to curl up in the large outdoor couch together to look at the stars. Since our first date on prom night, this was a regular occurrence for us to spend as many evenings as we could star gazing and just being together. Sometimes we would talk for hours about anything and everything, while other times there could be hours of silence with no awkwardness at all. We just fit together.

Tonight I made a wish, as I always did. I wished that I would always feel as cared for and loved as I did in this very moment.

That was the night that Mac and I were together for the first time, and everything about it was perfect. I realized that this was exactly how it was supposed to feel when you shared yourself with someone completely.

I woke up before him and lay there studying his face and thinking about all of the times we had shared as friends before this and wondered if there were signs all along that I could've missed. It didn't really matter now. We were here, and I knew this was exactly where I wanted to be.

Somehow I expected to feel guilty because of Michael, but surprisingly I didn't. Michael's death brought us closer, but if I really thought about it, Mac and I always had a special bond between us.

He would be leaving in just a few short weeks for his first semester in Waco, and I couldn't help but wonder what would happen to us when he left. I was enrolled at the University of Houston as a psychology major and he was going to Baylor on a football scholarship and would be majoring in economics and finance. We hadn't yet discussed our relationship and how things would play out once we were separated in the fall.

I started to get out of bed to make my way to the kitchen to brew coffee, but I barely began to move and felt his hands on my skin.

"Good morning, babe. Don't tell me you came to your senses and decided to make a quick getaway while I was still asleep?" He grinned at me with that gorgeous smile of his, hair slightly messy and eyes sparkling. Before I knew it, his arms were wrapped around me and my legs were tangled up in between his and the sheets. I was wearing his t-shirt, and the smell of him was absolutely intoxicating. There was no doubt that I was completely in love with him.

"You're never getting rid of me," I smiled and kissed him deeply.

He broke from our kiss and held my face in his hands. "I can promise you that I never will let you go. I love you, Linds."

We had the most amazing weekend together, and I didn't want it to end. As we packed up our things and loaded the Jeep, I couldn't help but think about how much I was going to miss him when he left.

On the ride back home, he held my hand while we listened to music and just simply enjoyed our time together. I was soaking up every minute of him that I could before we had to separate.

"Mac, what's going to happen when you leave for Waco?" I stared out the window waiting for his reply.

He brought my hand to his lips and softly pressed them against my skin. "Lindsey, nothing is going to happen. Things aren't going to change with us unless we let them, and I have no intentions of letting anything come between us. It's not going to be a goodbye, it's just a see ya soon."

I felt a tear roll down my cheek and I kept my face turned away from him so he couldn't see.

"Look at me," he said. I looked at him and smiled. "I mean it when I say that I love you, and I've never been happier."

"I love you too." I had my answer, and I trusted him with my heart. "The last thing I would want to do is hold you back from living your life at school."

Mac laughed a little. "You're not holding me back from anything. I'll be busy with football and classes, and you'll be working and taking classes so we will have to try and make time to see each other when we can. Is that going to work for you, or is that not what you want?" His tone had changed from playful to more serious.

"Mac, I want this to work for us. I'll miss you terribly, but we will get through it." I knew in my heart that this was right.

Two weeks later, we said a very tearful goodbye, or as he referred to it, 'see ya soon' and I watched him drive away from my house with his Jeep packed full of belongings for his dorm room. Along with the clothes, blankets and pillows, mini fridge, and other dorm necessities, he took a piece of my heart when he left. I had faith in our relationship, but that didn't help the fact that I missed him already and he wasn't even out of my sight yet.

Over the next few weeks I settled into a brand new routine. I was now living full-time at Keri's parents' house since my mom was moving north of Houston to Tomball and it was just too far of a commute for me to work and school. Classes started for the fall semester and I was getting into a good routine of Monday, Wednesday and Friday classes leaving Tuesdays, Thursdays, and the weekends for working.

I had taken a hostessing job during my junior year at an upscale steakhouse in Katy called Perry's and after I turned eighteen they trained me to start waitressing. The money was fantastic and the clientele was upscale, making it a great place to work and put myself through college.

Between a full class schedule and working four nights a week, I stayed busy enough to not go crazy missing Mac. We had decided that I would try to get up to see him one weekend a month, since it was harder for him to get home this fall because of his football schedule. In the spring he would make the trips home to see me once football was over. We talked nearly every day and texted constantly, and our relationship was thriving.

Melissa

ylan's proposal was something out of a romance novel last night. I lay in bed this morning on my day off staring at my finger and the shiny ring he placed on it. It was exactly what I wanted, and so was he. When Kyle proposed to me I knew it wasn't right. I had already known that I was going to end things with him because Dylan was the one I belonged with.

We didn't have much of a chance to talk last night about the engagement, or any wedding plans at all for that matter. Once Dylan and I got home, we opened a small bottle of champagne to toast before I slipped into something sexy and we made love more passionately than we ever had before.

Before he left this morning he kissed me goodbye and promised that over the weekend we would spend some time discussing details and start making some plans. I knew he wouldn't want to rush the wedding, and I was also in no hurry. I had always wanted a fall wedding, so I would talk to Dylan about the following fall for a date giving us almost a year and a half to plan.

I had a few days off, so I thought I would make a nice dinner tonight and we could enjoy a quiet night at home talking over some details. Then tomorrow maybe he would want to go home so we could see his mom and tell her the good news in person. Dylan was always very standoffish about bringing me back home to Katy. I never questioned why, but sometimes I wondered if maybe there was something, or someone, that maybe he didn't want me to discover. Whatever it was, we had only gone a few times to visit his mom together, so I didn't know her well at all.

My family would be thrilled and I couldn't wait for us to tell them together on Sunday, as my family had brunch almost every Sunday after church. This week I wanted to join them so we could surprise them with the news.

When Dylan got home from work, I had lasagna in the oven, a Caesar salad prepared and chilling in the fridge, and a bottle of Chianti, our favorite, ready for opening.

He came through the door with a wide smile on his face. "Hello my fiancé."

I greeted him at the door with a long, romantic kiss and felt my entire body tingle as I thought about the fact that I was going to be his wife. "Hello my future husband!" I was beaming and if I could've run through the streets screaming it to the world that I was engaged, I would've. I threw my arms around his neck and smothered him with kisses all over his face.

"I could get used to this if that's how you're going to greet your husband when he comes home from work." He scooped me up and set me down on the couch continuing with the display of affection. "How's my future bride doing today?"

"I'm on cloud nine!" I gushed happiness and I didn't want this amazing feeling to ever go away. "I've got dinner in the oven, so how about a glass of wine while we wait for it?"

"Perfect. I'm going to change out of these work clothes quick and I'll be right back to join you." He kissed me and went off to our room to change while I poured two glasses of wine for us and sat on the patio out back. July in Texas was normally not suitable weather for sitting outside but the temperature and humidity were both lower than normal this week and there was a gorgeous refreshing breeze.

He came outside to join me and we toasted to our engagement. It was the happiest I had ever been in my life to this point.

"So have you given any thought to when you want to get married?" I asked, hoping that we were going to be on the same page with this part at least.

"As long as you don't say next week or next month, I think I'll be good with whatever you are thinking."

I smiled, slightly relieved that he wasn't going to say that he wanted a long engagement. "Well, I've always wanted a fall wedding, so I was thinking end of October or early November of next year. That'll give us over a year to save and plan for it. What do you think?"

He reached for my hand and brought it to his lips to kiss it, "I think it sounds perfect."

"Have you told your mom yet?"

"Not yet. I thought I should tell her in person instead of over the phone. I was thinking I'd maybe make a quick trip home tomorrow and spend the day with her and tell her over dinner."

And there it was…again. Always wanting to go home by himself, never inviting me. The last thing I wanted to do was pick a fight with him tonight. This was supposed to be a happy time, and I didn't want to ruin it, but I needed to know why I was never asked to be a part of his life back home.

"How about I go with you so we can tell her together?" I thought this was a better way of broaching the subject than to start making accusations or harp on him for not asking me to go with him.

He seemed a little uneasy and taken back by my asking to go with him, "Oh, sorry. I guess I just figured since I always go by myself that I'd just make it a quick visit myself."

"Well Dylan, that's how it's always been, and I'm thinking maybe we could start to make the trip together. I'd like to get to know your mom better, and know more about where you grew up." I was waiting for the rebuttal, but surprisingly it didn't come.

"Okay, let's leave early in the morning so we can spend some time with her and have an early dinner before we head back home. Are we having brunch with your parents on Sunday so we can tell everyone?"

Wow…who is this man and what did he do to Dylan?

I was shocked. "Yeah, that sounds great about tomorrow. And yes, Sunday I was thinking we'd join them for brunch when they get out of church." It made me happy that he wanted to take me with him tomorrow to see his mom.

"I'll go call mom and tell her we're coming tomorrow. Want me to check on dinner while I'm inside?"

Again, who was this man? I could really get used to this new Dylan. "Sure, that would be great!"

He went inside and I closed my eyes to feel the evening sun on my face. I had everything I wanted at that very moment. My career was on its way, we had a great home, and now I was engaged to the man I love.

Dylan

We got on the road around 9 A.M. Saturday morning to drive to Katy and see mom for the day. Our plan was to tell her about the engagement and then take her to dinner to celebrate. The drive home was quicker than it usually felt, most likely due to the fact that I had a copilot this time unlike most of my solo trips.

I knew that Melissa felt like I never wanted to bring her home with me, and she was partially right. In the beginning it was mainly because when I came home to see mom, I just wanted to spend one-on-one time with her. I didn't want to have to help make small talk between Mom and Melissa. Mom and I had our routine and it worked for us.

But now Melissa was going to be a part of my life forever, so I needed to find a way to interject her into the dynamic. She didn't share our love for baseball, so I'd have to try and find something for her and Mom to bond over.

"I'm so excited to tell your mom that we're getting married! Do you think she will be happy for us?"

I could completely understand why she was asking this right now. My mom barely knew Melissa and that was my fault.

"Of course she will be. She likes you, and the more she gets to know you, the more she will love you...just like I do." I felt guilty for not encouraging a relationship between the two most important women in my life until this point, but there was another reason for not bringing Melissa home more often. Lindsey.

I suppose I was keeping my life back home separate from my life in College Station because I needed a clear line drawn between the two. What happened with Lindsey was something I still thought about and I would probably always wonder what would've happened if the events of that weekend had turned out differently. But they didn't, and this was the direction my life was going now.

I'd stopped asking Rachel about Lindsey because I thought that it was best for me to just stay gone from her life. The more I knew about what she was doing, the more I was tempted to contact her.

By now, Lindsey would have been done with her first year of college, wherever she ended up going. Whatever she was doing, I always hoped that she was doing well. And some nights, I'd look up at the sky, find a star, and make a wish for her.

We arrived at Mom's late morning around eleven, and although she knew we were coming, she was still so excited to see us as if we had surprised her with our visit. She hugged us both and brought us in the house for a light lunch and some coffee.

"I'm so happy you're BOTH here this time." She shot me a look and then turned to Melissa and smiled. "I'm guessing that it's my son's fault that you don't come to visit with him, am I right Melissa?"

Melissa grinned and looked at me. "Well, I hope that's going to change and I'll be making more trips here with him from now on."

"So Mom, Melissa and I have some news we want to share with you. We're getting married." I waited for her reaction, knowing that she would be thrilled to be gaining a daughter-in-law, but slightly upset with me for not even mentioning the idea to her before now.

Mom reached out to Melissa with her arms open wide, "Oh you two! I'm so happy for you both!" She hugged Melissa and I got the look from her over her shoulder that told me she and I would be having a private discussion at a later date.

Melissa showed her the ring and they cackled like hens for the next half hour discussing everything from dresses and tuxedos to sit down dinner or hors d'oeuvres. It made me feel awful that I had been keeping the two of them apart all of these years because of my own issues. Mom only had me all these years, so now she was gaining a daughter, and by the look on her face she was more than ecstatic.

After lunch I decided to go for a bike ride while the two of them continued their conversation about roses versus hydrangeas for wedding bouquets.

As I rode around the subdivision I instinctively rode down the street that Lindsey and Rachel grew up on, and in front of their house to my surprise was a for sale sign with a pending rider on it. I had no idea that their mom was selling the house and moving. Rachel and I were still friends, but we didn't see each other as much anymore now that she and Troy had bought a house in Austin and were both working.

I could tell by the absence of curtains on the windows and the stack of newspapers piled up on the front steps that they had already moved out. Where was Lindsey now?

I stopped for a moment and stood at the end of the driveway. Rachel and I had a lot of good memories swimming in the pool out back, watching movies, and sneaking her in and out of her window to go to parties after her curfew. But the memories that were flooding my mind right now were of Lindsey. The night I walked her home and kissed her for the first time, and the first and only time we had been together was here in this house.

Lindsey and I never had a chance to see if we could've been something together. Fate took over that weekend and had another plan for us. Whatever path she was on now, I only hoped that she was happy.

I turned and headed home, my mind preoccupied with thoughts of Lindsey and where she was and what she was doing now. For the past two years I had wondered why she never reached out to me again, and couldn't stop kicking myself for not trying to call her. I thought I was doing the right thing by giving her some space. I just didn't realize at the time that I gave her too much.

When I got back to mom's house I showered and changed for an early dinner. We wanted to eat by five p.m. so we could head back home by seven. I let mom make the decision of where we would eat, as I always did when I came to visit. Usually she wanted to go for either Mexican food at Larry's or to Willie G's for her favorite red snapper dish. But she said that tonight was a special occasion so she wanted to try a place that she was hearing a lot of great reviews about.

Our reservation was for five o'clock and we were seated as soon as we arrived. Since it was so early, the restaurant wasn't very busy. It was an upscale steakhouse and the intoxicating smells were making our mouths water as we starting reviewing the menus once we were seated. I left the table to use the restroom and told Melissa to go ahead and order me something to drink, just a beer since I would be driving home in a few hours.

179

When I returned to the table, mom and Melissa were chatting like old friends.

Mom turned to me, "Dylan, you're never going to believe who is our waitress!"

"No idea mom, who?"

"Your friend Rachel's sister, Lindsey. Do you remember her? I don't think she recognized me though."

The color must've gone out of my face and I thought I was going to pass out. How could this be happening?

Melissa was watching me and I had to recover so she wouldn't see that I was clearly shaken by this. "Dylan, are you ok?"

Snap out of it.

"Yeah, um sure I remember her. Of course, I mean, I was at their house all the time with Rachel when we were in school." I knew I would have to get it together or Melissa was going to start asking questions.

"Sweet girl. Such a shame about her boyfriend that died in that car accident. Remember that Dylan? It was a few years ago, so sad. He was a good boy too from what everyone said."

Now my blood was starting to boil at hearing this comment. 'Good boy'…not exactly mom. "I remember the accident. He wasn't such a great guy mom."

My mom looked surprised at my comment, "Dylan, that's not a nice thing to say about him. What happened to him was a horrible tragedy."

By now Melissa was looking at me oddly because she knew me well enough to know that something was going on and there was more to this than I was saying.

"Yes mom, it was unfortunate." I wanted to disappear and leave before Lindsey came back to the table. It would no doubt be awkward for her to come back and see me sitting here. And we were here to celebrate our engagement, which would make things even more uncomfortable, maybe not for her but for me. The last thing I wanted was for Melissa to pick up on anything going on between me and Lindsey.

I glanced toward the bar and saw her standing there at the service area putting our drinks onto her cocktail tray to make her way over to us, unknowingly walking into a situation that she was not expecting. I watched her walk toward our area of the restaurant smiling at other patrons as she came across the floor.

She was beautiful, and I couldn't take my eyes off her as she approached. When she was about ten feet away she looked straight at me and froze as our eyes met for the first time since the night we said goodbye at the hospital.

There was no way that Melissa wasn't picking up on this right now. Lindsey looked at me, then at Melissa, and back at me.

"Oh Lindsey, look, you remember Dylan right?" My mom had no idea that she was putting us both in a very uncomfortable situation right now.

Lindsey recovered with a slight smile, obviously assessing the situation and realizing who Melissa was and what we were doing here for dinner.

"Yes, I remember him." She looked at me and smiled, "How are you Dylan?"

I knew I would have to play along with this if I was going to survive the next couple hours. "Hey Lindsey, I'm good thanks. How are you doing?"

"Good. Great actually. I just finished my first year at U of H and it went really well." I could tell she was uncomfortable and I felt terrible that she was being caught off guard by our being here.

Lindsey was setting our drinks down as my mom started again, "We're celebrating tonight! Dylan is getting married!"

And there it was. I wanted to get up and run out there as fast as I could right now.

Lindsey looked like someone had just slapped her in the face. If I could've apologized, I would've.

Still, Melissa just sat there ping ponging her gaze from me to Lindsey and back again. The ride home would no doubt be two hours of interrogations. It was impossible to not see that there was something more going on here.

Gracefully, Lindsey turned to me and then to Melissa, "Congratulations to you both." I watched her glance down at Melissa's hand and then back up to her face again as she was continuing to process the situation.

Melissa finally spoke, "How long has it been since you two have seen each other?" She gave me a look and I knew that she was fishing for something.

Lindsey and I caught each other's eyes and quickly looked away from each other again.

She spoke up before I could say anything, "It's been a couple of years I guess."

This was true, but it wasn't all of the truth really. I needed to find a way to get through this dinner and prepare myself for the long ride back home with Melissa tonight.

"Can we order? Do you two know what you want for dinner?" I was trying to get mom and Melissa away from the conversation of Lindsey and me and make this as easy on her as possible.

Melissa wasn't going to let this go so easily though. "So, did you see each other that weekend that I was out of town and you came home to help a friend?" She was glaring at me now and I knew she was putting the pieces together based on the awkwardness we were all feeling.

She knew I was in town that weekend, but I lied about why I was there. I had told her a friend needed help moving some furniture.

Lindsey looked horrified as she turned her gaze to me and waited for me to answer Melissa's question.

"We did see each other that weekend. I stopped at a party at a friend's house Friday night while I was in town and she was there. So yes, we saw each other that weekend." My tone was starting to change and although I owed Melissa an explanation, this was not the time or the place for us to have the conversation. "Can we just order dinner?"

"I'll just give y'all a few minutes." Lindsey couldn't get away from our table fast enough, and really I couldn't blame her.

Mom seemed confused, "I don't understand, is there a problem that you ran into each other that weekend at a party? I didn't even know you were in town Dylan. Why didn't you stop at the house or at least tell me you were coming home that weekend?"

The last thing I wanted to do was upset my mother. "Mom, it was a last minute trip home to help a friend move his furniture and I just spent the weekend hanging with him and a few other friends from school."

Melissa got up from the table, "Will y'all excuse me for a minute? I need some fresh air." She hurried away from the table and I watched her bolt through the front doors of the restaurant.

I knew I needed to talk to her, so I apologized to mom and followed her outside into the parking lot. She was fuming, and I knew she had already put the pieces together.

"Liss, this isn't what you think it is."

She turned and snapped, "Really? Well then I'd really love to hear your explanation as to what it is then Dylan, because you don't need to be a genius to figure out that there's something you're not telling me. The two of you aren't exactly being subtle about whatever the hell is going on between you."

"She's Rachel's sister. Rachel is my best friend, and when I got to town that weekend and ran into her at the party, she had been in a fight with her boyfriend Michael. A really bad fight and I was worried that he might come to her house so I didn't want her to be alone. So, um, I stayed there with her Friday night."

Again, not the complete truth, but the last thing I wanted to do was hurt her for something that was over before it began.

"So you spent the night with her?"

"Not like you are thinking. I slept in the recliner and she slept on the couch." There, that part was one hundred percent true.

"Oh, so that makes it totally okay that you spent the night with someone? And that you lied to me about it."

I knew I had to figure out a way to end this conversation so we could salvage this night with mom. "I didn't lie to you about it. I just didn't tell you everything because I didn't want you to read more into it than what it was. Can we please just go inside and have dinner with mom and discuss this later?"

She couldn't even look at me as she turned and walked back into the restaurant. I trailed behind her with my tail between my legs. This evening couldn't end fast enough.

"I'm sorry mom. We just had a little misunderstanding and we needed to talk privately for a minute."

Melissa was still uncomfortable and I could tell she was just putting on a good front for my mom, and no doubt going to turn on the show for Lindsey.

No one was more uneasy than we were though, as Lindsey and I could barely look at each other. My feelings for her had not changed, whatever they actually were, but I was in love with Melissa and she was my future. Still, seeing her, I couldn't help but think of how things could've been so different if the events of that weekend had gone another way.

Lindsey came to the table to get our dinner order, and she quickly exited making no idle chitchat, strictly business. Melissa and mom continued their conversation about wedding plans and I just sat in silence mostly just trying to process my thoughts. I would tell Melissa the truth, and hope that she could get past it and still want to be with me.

The appetizers, salads, dinners, and desserts seemed to take an eternity tonight, simply because I wanted to be anywhere but here right now.

Just before dessert, I excused myself to use the restroom again. I needed a minute to be alone. As I crossed through the restaurant to the other side of the bar toward the restrooms, Lindsey was standing with her back to me in the waitress station.

I came up behind her and touched her on the shoulder, not meaning to startle her like I did.

"I'm sorry, I just wanted to…um, I really don't know what I wanted to say. I had no idea you worked here."

"It's ok. It's just, strange I guess, seeing you again after all this time. After… well, since we, were together."

I wanted so badly to put my arms around her, but I knew I couldn't. She was even more beautiful than the last time I saw her. The last couple years had given her a matured look, yet to me she was still fragile and delicate.

"Lindsey, I want you to know that I really wanted to be with you. I had no intentions of that being a one time thing between us. But I thought you needed some time to grieve and sort through your feelings so I wanted to give you the space to do that. Then I never heard from you again."

She let her eyes drop as if she couldn't look at me. "I'm sorry Dylan. I had so much guilt over what happened to Michael that I just felt like if I called you that I'd be betraying him all over again."

"You didn't betray him and you have nothing to feel guilty about Linds."

"I know that now, but at the time I was overwhelmed and it took me awhile to get to a place where I could let go of the guilt. By then, I guess I figured you'd moved on. And it looks like I was right."

She seemed hurt, and that was the last thing I wanted.

"Lindsey, I don't know what to say." I reached for her hand, "I wanted to be with you. Please don't ever think that it wasn't you that I wanted. I should've reached out to you again and not let you go. I'm so sorry."

She looked directly into my eyes, her hazel eyes now filling with tears, "Are you happy?" she asked.

I didn't want to hurt her, but I couldn't lie to her either.

"I am."

A single tear fell down her cheek and landed on my hand as I was still holding hers.

She smiled at me, "Then if you're happy, I'm happy for you."

I reached up and wiped the streak of teardrop off her cheek. All of a sudden we were back in time, two years ago, on the porch at her house. I knew I should leave but I was frozen in place, just like I was that night.

"Lindsey, I hope you find your happiness someday too. You deserve it." I leaned in and kissed her on that single freckle on the end of her nose.

I went back to the table feeling better that I had gotten the opportunity to have a few minutes alone with Lindsey. It didn't change the fact that I was kicking myself for not reaching out to her, and for just letting her go like I did. The connection between us was undeniable. It could've been because we never got the chance to explore a relationship with each other, so there were so many unknowns and "what ifs". Or maybe there was really something between us. Either way, fate had pulled us in different directions. The events of that weekend changed our course, and there was nothing we could do now to change it even if we wanted to.

Once dinner was over we drove mom back home and said our goodbyes to start our long drive. I was dreading the next two hours with Melissa knowing that we would have to try and work through this ordeal. I couldn't believe that we had just gotten engaged and already this was happening.

We drove without saying a word for the first half hour until I finally broke the silence.

"So, do you want to talk about it?"

Melissa turned to me, "I'm not sure what you want me to say. I just found out that my fiancé who I've been engaged to for about a minute lied to me about spending the night with someone else two years ago." She turned and looked out the window again. "So, I don't think you could blame me for not having anything to say to you right now."

"Melissa, I told you, it wasn't like that. She's like a sister to me and I just wanted to be there in case she needed me."

Saying these words almost made me sick to my stomach. I didn't see Lindsey as a sister at all, but I had to try and make Melissa move on without prying more into this. It was once, one time that I let myself get caught up in the moment. I couldn't call it a mistake, because I didn't feel like it was at the time, and I still don't.

"Dylan, did you sleep with her? Just tell me the truth. I'd rather know the truth now and figure out how to deal with it than find out sometime down the road that not only did you sleep with her, but that you lied to me on top of it."

I couldn't believe I was about to do this, but I was going to tell her the truth. If I lost her because of this, then at least I would know that I had been honest. We could go our separate ways, or we could move ahead into a marriage with no secrets or lies.

"I went home that Friday night with intentions of just making sure she was ok."

Melissa looked confused. "I don't understand. Why would she not be okay and why would it be any business of yours anyway?"

"I'm sorry. I wanted to tell you the truth when I got back that weekend, but I just didn't know how. That Friday night I was playing cards with Troy at Rachel's apartment, when you were out of town for your girls weekend, and Rachel got a call that Michael had been physically abusive to her and she was home alone and scared."

"I still don't know how that had anything at all to do with you Dylan."

"So, a year before that, I had gone home for the weekend and I ran into her at a party. She was drinking and was going to walk home alone, but I stopped her because I didn't think it was safe for her to be out at night like that by herself. Rachel is my best friend, and I didn't want to see something happen to her little sister."

Melissa was getting irritated as I was not quite getting to the point, "Again, your problem because why?"

"I walked her to her house, we had both had a few drinks, and we kissed. Just once, that's all it was. I don't know why I did it, I guess we just kinda got caught up in a moment." I paused for a minute trying to figure out how to explain all of this without letting Melissa discover that I really had true feelings for Lindsey. "I didn't have any contact with her for almost a year after that night." That part was completely true. "But when I heard about what Michael had done that night, I just for some reason decided to make sure she was okay and that she wasn't alone in case he came back."

"Dylan, I was out of town and you were off chasing around some girl?" She was furious, and I couldn't blame her.

"I know, that's what it sounds like, and I'm sorry, but there is a history with Lindsey and her family. She's not just 'some girl' Melissa."

"Well, then tell me exactly what she means to you that she's so special you would risk our relationship."

"I can't explain it because I really don't know. I just felt like I needed to be there for her. To protect her. So I came home and tried to find her. She wasn't at her house so I had a feeling she would be at a party down the road, and I was right. When I got there she was spinning out of control and having a panic attack. I took her back to her house and stayed with her. I slept in the recliner and she slept on the couch."

"You didn't answer my question. Did you have sex with her?"

She was crying and I reached for her hand but she pulled away. The last thing I wanted to do was hurt her, especially now that we finally were happy and had everything we wanted.

"The next day, she broke down and I was comforting her." I had no idea how she was going to react to this when I told her the rest, but I knew I had to tell her the truth. "It wasn't something either of us expected or planned in any way."

She turned and glared at me, "Well, then that just makes it all okay then. Since you didn't mean for it to happen, then I guess it's not a big deal right?"

"Melissa, I'm so sorry. It only happened once, and I wanted to tell you but I just didn't know how. I had no idea if it was just a one-time thing, or if something would come of it. So I said nothing."

As soon as I said the words I knew I had screwed up. She was going to think she was just the consolation prize because Lindsey didn't want me.

"So, let me get this straight. You slept with her, then just came home to me like nothing happened? But if she wanted to be with you then you were going to leave me? For her?" She laughed, but there was nothing she found funny about this.

"I don't know how to make you understand but I'm trying. I was with her when she got the call later that day that about Michael's accident. I took her to the hospital and stayed with her for awhile. Then I came back home the next morning. We never even got a chance to talk about what happened or figure out what it meant to either of us."

"Wow. Do you want me to feel bad for you that you never got to find out how your little story with her ended?" She was sarcastic and taking jabs at me. I deserved every bit of it too.

"No, of course not. I'm just trying to make you realize why I never said anything to you. I just wanted to come home and try and figure it all out. We never spoke again after that until today."

I realized that this wasn't making anything better, and if anything it was making it much worse.

Melissa was silent for what felt like an eternity. I could only imagine she was trying to process all of this and I'm sure it wasn't easy for her. She stared out the window and we didn't speak again until we were about a half hour from home.

My mind was swirling with thoughts of what would become of us now that the truth was out on the table. I didn't want to lose her. I loved her and wanted to share my life with her. But still, I couldn't help thinking maybe she was right. Would I have left her if Lindsey had wanted me back then? I didn't know the answer to that question, and I never would.

Lindsey

I have had some horrible nights at work, but this one really takes the top prize for the worst ever. It's been two years since I've seen or heard from him and now that I'm finally feeling happy and like my life is together, he waltzes in the restaurant with his new fiancé?

It was hard to be mad at him for coming into the restaurant when he had no idea I was working there, but still it didn't make anything about it easier.

All I wanted to do was finish work and go see Mac. He was home for the summer from Baylor and we were both just working and trying to spend as much time together as possible. We both had a good first year, and our relationship was prospering even though we were away from each other most of the time. There was trust, respect, and so much love for each other that it made the separation easier to handle for us both.

I had been honest with Mac from the beginning about Dylan and what happened between us in the past, so I would of course tell him about tonight. When I got done with my shift I drove to his parents house a few miles away. They were on an Alaskan cruise so I was going to stay with him while they were gone. I let myself in the door and found him in the kitchen making a snack.

He greeted me with a kiss as usual. "Hey babe, how was work?"

I groaned.

"Wow. That bad, huh?" He wrapped me up in an enormous hug and immediately I started feeling calm and peaceful again. "Sit down and I'll make us both a snack and we can talk about it."

I smiled as I looked up at him, still in his arms. This was my happy place, with him. He had become my world and I knew my heart and my life were always safe with Mac.

"That sounds perfect. I'm going to change out of this uniform and I'll tell you all about it." I hurried off to his room and threw on some comfy clothes. When I returned he was on the couch with a platter of nachos and a couple iced teas for us.

"So what happened, Linds? Tell me you didn't get another one of those Red Hat Ladies groups with twenty separate checks again?" He laughed, knowing that a group of old ladies with separate checks was one of the biggest pet peeves of mine.

"Actually I would've preferred the old ladies with separate checks."

"Ouch! Must've been really bad then."

"Dylan came in for dinner. With his mother. And his fiancé."

He wasn't smiling anymore. A look of worry came across his face as he turned to me sitting next to him on the couch.

"Oh, wow, that's kind of out of the blue isn't it? Did you have to wait on them?"

I nodded. "It was really awkward, Mac. He's engaged to Melissa. She was his girlfriend when—well, you know." Suddenly I felt ashamed and embarrassed that I had been the kind of person to sleep with another woman's boyfriend. "I couldn't even look at her."

Mac took my hand, "Linds, it was a long time ago. You have nothing to feel bad about. I'm sorry if it was uncomfortable for you though. I know that you had feelings for him." He paused, "Do you still?"

I quickly responded, "No, not at all. I did, but that was two years ago and everything has changed since then." I wouldn't let Mac know that my heart skipped and my entire body went numb when I laid eyes on Dylan for the first time in two years. I couldn't tell him that part of me still ached for him and wondered whether or not we could've had a future together if things had turned out differently that weekend.

"But at one point you did, and I'm sure it was still hard to see him today."

Mac was my boyfriend, but above all, he was my best friend and had been for as long as I could remember. He knew me better than just about anyone and I couldn't hide my feelings from him.

"I don't know what I did to deserve you, but I'm so thankful for you. Thank you for understanding and not making this into more than it is." I kissed him and settled in on the couch next to him. He was watching TV and had already gotten past the conversation about Dylan. That was one of the things I loved about Mac the most, he didn't let anything bother him or dwell on things that didn't matter.

He wasn't thinking about Dylan anymore, but I was. I imagined he was defending himself right now to her about me and what happened between us. I had no idea if he would tell her the truth, and what she would do if he told her everything. Regardless of what happened with their relationship, I was where I needed, and wanted to be. Nothing would change that, not even Dylan.

Melissa

I've heard people talk about hindsight before, and now I could almost write a book on it. If I had know that Dylan was planning to leave me, would it have affected my decision? Would I have chosen to take a chance with Kyle or would I have fought to keep Dylan from leaving me for her?

I couldn't believe this was happening right now. Two days ago, he had proposed to me in the most romantic way I could have ever imagined, and now he just told me that he cheated on me two years ago.

Yet, as I sit here trying to figure out what to say to him, I can't help but think of what a hypocrite I am. What I had done was even worse than what he's telling me now. I carried on a relationship with someone else and let it continue for months behind his back.

As much as this hurt, how could I leave him when I had done the same thing? Should I tell him about Kyle? No. That would destroy us. Lindsey was a one time thing right? He didn't have feelings for her, so we could just move past it.

After about an hour I broke the silence between us. I had questions that I needed answered in order to move past this.

"Did you have feelings for her? Do you still?" I almost wasn't sure I wanted the answers.

"I did, yes. But it was over before it started."

I knew he was being honest with me. "What about when you saw her today? Did you feel anything?"

It took him a few minutes to answer.

193

"Yes, but let me explain before you jump to conclusions. I always looked at her as my best friend's little sister until three years ago. When I saw her today, she was different again. She's been through a lot, and I'm happy to see that she's doing well. I care about her and what happens to her, but that is where it ends."

"What if she still wanted to be with you? Would that change anything for you?"

"No, it wouldn't. I'm in love with you and we are planning a future together."

He reached for my hand and I let him take it. I knew he loved me, and after what I had done to him I couldn't hold this against him. I could be sad, hurt, and angry for awhile, but I would have to let it go and get over it.

"Thank you for being honest with me."

"Liss, I'm so sorry for hurting you. Please believe me when I say that it happened once, and it will never happen again. I love you so much."

"I love you too. I just need a little time to wrap my head around it."

"Do you think you can forgive me?"

I knew I had to forgive him. I had to forgive myself for what I had done too. We were both human, and we made mistakes.

"Yes."

We didn't speak again until we got home. All we could do was say goodnight as we got into bed and moved to opposite sides, an odd gesture for a couple that had just gotten engaged forty eight hours ago. I was hurting because of what he had done, and what I had done. He was no doubt hurting too.

I lay there thinking about what he had done. He was in bed with her, while I was with Kyle. I deserved this karma for what I had done. My heart was hurting now, but it was nothing compared to what Dylan would've felt if he had found out about Kyle and me.

"Dylan?" I whispered.

He was still awake, "What is it?"

"If you loved me back then, why were you drawn to her?" I felt the tears start to fall down my face.

He turned over toward me, "I did love you then, and I love you now."

I moved into his arms and let him hold me as I cried. The tears weren't just for me and the pain I was feeling because of Lindsey. They were my tears for what I had done to him, even without him knowing, it still hurt me. I had no regret that I stayed with Dylan and walked away from Kyle. The regret I was feeling now was for letting myself be drawn away from Dylan to begin with. I was searching for something that I wasn't finding with him at the time. If I had just been patient, it would've come to me.

"Tell me what I need to do to make this up to you. I promise you I will never let something like this happen again."

"I just want to always be your first choice. Please don't ever put anyone or anything in front of me, in front of us, ever again. We can get past this. I know we can."

He kissed me on the forehead and held me tighter. I knew that as much as this hurt, I had to get past it.

I fell asleep in his arms and woke in the morning to the smell of coffee brewing in the kitchen. I pulled on a robe and went to find him. He was on the back patio and I could see him from the window. I thought about joining him, but I just sat for a minute watching him. I loved him fiercely and I wanted so badly to be his wife. In the kitchen the coffeemaker beeped signaling the end of the brew cycle. I made us both a cup and went to sit with him outside in the warm morning sunshine.

"Good morning." He must've been deep in thought because I startled him as I spoke. "Where did you go?"

"Hey, nowhere…just sitting here thinking."

"I meant where were you just now, you seem to be a million miles away." I could only hope that he wasn't thinking of her right now.

He reached out to take the cup from my hand as I extended it to him. "Thanks. I was going to bring some in to you."

"Are you ok? You look preoccupied."

"Yeah, I'm good. Just thinking about last night."

"If you had to go back, would you still have done what you did?" Why did I ask a question that I really didn't want to know the answer to?

"I guess that depends." He replied.

I was stunned. "What do you mean?"

"Well, while I was with Lindsey you were with Kyle. So I guess it would depend on whether or not you were still seeing him."

I froze. All I could do is stare straight at him.

"How, how do you know about him?" Was this really happening or was I still asleep and having a nightmare? If he knew about Kyle, why didn't he ever say anything to me?

"I knew something was different with you when you stopped constantly focusing on our relationship and where it was going. You started taking "girls trips" and I never thought anything more of it until the last trip you took, when I ended up back in Katy with Lindsey. When I came back, I had planned to tell you about what I had done and face whatever consequences came with admitting the truth. I drove to the airport to surprise you."

I felt like I was going to be sick. He must've seen me with Kyle at the airport. Oh God, why didn't he say anything?

"I watched you kiss him in the airport parking lot."

"Dylan…" I tried to speak but there was nothing I could say. The words wouldn't come out.

"You don't need to say anything. We're even I guess." He was angry, and I could tell his tone was sarcastic and mean.

"No, we aren't. We both screwed up, but you told me the truth last night. Would you have ever told me if we hadn't run into her yesterday?"

"No. I wouldn't have said a word. And I never would've told you that I knew about Kyle. At the time I figured we both made mistakes and we could just move past them. What was done was done and there was no changing what happened. So I decided to keep it all to myself and push it down."

"I should've told you about Kyle."

He turned to look me in the eyes. "Last night I waited for you to say something and be honest about what you had done, but you didn't."

"Dylan, I was so scared. I didn't want to lose you. That was the last time I saw him, I swear. I knew I had made a huge mistake. I'm so sorry."

"Last night you could've told me." He paused and gave me a half smile, "I guess that's why you were so quick to tell me we could get past this. You had your own guilt."

I could hardly believe that this is how we were spending our first weekend as a newly engaged couple. We should've been celebrating our crazy insane love and dancing around the living room naked.

"I don't know what to say to you. I could try and tell you all of the reasons that I had an affair with Kyle, but they would just be excuses. The bottom line is I screwed up. I was unhappy and looking to feel better about myself, and instead of coming to you and talking to you I turned to someone else. I'm so sorry."

I put my head in my hands and sobbed. All I wanted was to go back to the Lake and his proposal and forget about the past twenty-four hours. Dylan got up and went inside leaving me crying on the patio. In that moment I was scared. Scared to death that he would leave me. What I had done was so much worse than the one time he had betrayed me. Not only did I carry on an affair, but I had the opportunity to come clean last night about it and instead I made him feel guilty for his indiscretions and never took responsibility for my own.

We were supposed to be meeting my family in just a few short hours to tell them about our engagement and celebrate with them. I didn't know how to face them alone. They had to be expecting big news from us because we never joined them for brunch unless it was a special occasion.

I wiped my tears away and turned to go inside, but just as I started to stand up from my chair I heard the door open and looked up to see him standing there. He was holding the box that my engagement ring was in the night he proposed. My heart sank. He was taking my ring back. I looked at my hand, shaking, and looked up at him with tears in my eyes.

"Dylan, please, don't do this." I pleaded with him through the stream of tears coming now like waves.

He said nothing. I slowly removed the beautiful symbol of his love for me from my trembling finger and held it in the palm of my hand as I cried. I couldn't look at him as he retrieved it from my outstretched hand.

But then, just as he took it from my hand and I waited for him to turn and walk away, something else happened.

Dylan lowered himself once again to one knee, and took my hand in his.

"Melissa, neither of us is perfect. We've made mistakes and will likely make more over the years to come. But I love you, with all my heart, and I want us to recommit to each other. I want to vow to you to be faithful and honest, and to always make you happy. Will you take this ring, again, and re-affirm your promise to me that you'll do the same?"

I could barely see through my tears as I lowered myself to my knees and kissed his face.

"I love you Dylan.

Part Three

"Don't close the book,

just turn the page."

—unknown

Dylan

It would be several months before Melissa and I would be okay again, but we got to a good place eventually. We had a few more arguments, hurt feelings, and issues with trusting each other that we had to work through, but we loved each other and were both willing to do whatever it took to make it work. We had decided on a long engagement so we could work through things, but told everyone who asked that we just weren't in any hurry.

The following fall, when I saw the wedding invitation in the mail, I knew that the feelings we fought so hard to get past were going to surface again tonight when Melissa saw it. Rachel and Troy were getting married in a few months, and of course I was going to be on the guest list.

Nothing was ever said to Rachel about what had happened between Lindsey and me, and Melissa knew that I couldn't just end my friendship with Rachel. We had been friends for almost twenty years, and she and I had been through too much together for us to ever lose that connection.

Nonetheless, it was difficult for Melissa to be around Rachel sometimes knowing what she knew about Lindsey and me. But she knew that my friendship with her was important so she never made it an issue for us to still spend time with them.

The wedding would be a hard event for Melissa though, knowing that Lindsey would no doubt be in the wedding party. There was no way I would miss Rachel's wedding, no matter what the circumstances. Melissa's feelings were important to me of course, but Rachel was my oldest friend and that was important to me as well.

201

When Melissa came home from work, I had poured a couple glasses of wine for us already and had ordered Chinese for us so that we could take a night off from cooking. She knew that Rachel and Troy were engaged, but I don't think she knew that they had set a date. I did, but I never brought it up in conversation to her because I knew it would just cause her anxiety and stress.

So I waited until we had a chance to unwind on the couch with some vino before I brought up the subject of the envelope on the counter that I had conveniently set underneath a Men's Health magazine so she wouldn't see it.

"Hey, we got a wedding invitation in the mail today for Rachel and Troy." I was gingerly broaching the subject, waiting to see what her reaction would be.

She didn't have much of an expression, "Oh, I didn't realize they'd set a date? So when is the wedding?"

Her casual answer surprised me a little. "I didn't open it yet, so I don't actually know really." I got up and went to grab the invitation. I opened it and checked the date. "Looks like the first weekend in November."

She smiled, "You know how much I love a fall wedding."

I went to the couch and wrapped her up in my arms. "The next fall wedding we'll be at will be ours next year."

"We really need to set a date."

I was surprised to hear her say that because for the past year we hadn't talked much at all about the wedding or making any plans. We knew we were still moving toward marriage, but we were just trying to reconnect and get over what happened.

"Let's do that this weekend. I didn't want to push the subject because I wasn't sure if you were ready." I had been treading lightly about our relationship and letting her take the lead with everything. I knew that she turned to Kyle because I was unavailable to her and I wasn't giving her what she needed from me. But she knew that I had feelings for Lindsey that wouldn't just go away. I was with Lindsey because I was drawn to her, and I wanted her. That was hard for Melissa to forgive, and I couldn't blame her. I sometimes still struggled with those feelings too, but I'd never let her know. Hurting Melissa was the last thing I wanted.

Reluctantly she agreed that we should get out a calendar and plan a date for our wedding next year. We spent the rest of the evening watching tv and just enjoying the life we were planning together.

We agreed on a date for the following October and we decided that after Rachel's wedding we would start working on a location and the rest of the details.

She turned to me on the couch, "Will it be weird for you to see her again?"

I knew she was talking about Lindsey. And I also knew there was no right answer for that question. If I said 'yes' then she would be hurt thinking that I still had feelings for her, and if I said 'no' then she would probably know I was lying to her.

"I don't know, maybe a little. I don't want it to be awkward for you, and I don't want anything to upset Rachel's day. Are you going to be ok?"

She shrugged her shoulders, "I don't know. I guess I'm going to have to be okay with being there with her. It's not about any of us, it's about Rachel and Troy."

"I'm really sorry that this is going to bring the whole thing back up again." I was sorry for her, and for Lindsey. I knew she would be uncomfortable too, but it was unavoidable. In six weeks we'd all be together in the same church and at the same reception, and for the sake of the bride we had to put all of our feelings aside for the day.

She smiled at me, "It's ok. We'll be fine."

The day of the wedding, Melissa looked stunning in a floor length black dress with her nails, hair, and makeup perfectly done.

"Wow! You look absolutely gorgeous!" I stood staring at her with my mouth wide open as she came out of our bedroom.

"Awww, thanks babe." She smiled and kissed me on the cheek, then wiped away the lipstick she left there.

"You'll be the most beautiful woman there today." I was still staring at her and admiring how amazing she looked right now.

"Well, I'll be the second most beautiful woman there." She paused and I wondered if she was going to start worrying and being insecure about Lindsey. "Rachel, will be the most beautiful woman there."

Good, she wasn't going there.

"Of course she will be, to everyone else. But to me, it'll still be you." I leaned in and kissed her again, "Don't tell Rachel I said that though."

We left for the wedding, and in the pit of my stomach I was feeling the anxiousness and anticipation of seeing Lindsey again. My heart and my life was with Melissa, but somehow Lindsey would always have a piece of me, and a piece of my heart.

Lindsey

$\mathcal{I}$ knew my sister's wedding would be coming soon and after the last time I saw Dylan, the situation would no doubt be uncomfortable for all of us. Mac would be there with me as my date of course, but he was always so grounded and relaxed that I knew he wouldn't be the one feeling the awkwardness.

As a bridesmaid, I would be preoccupied and busy at the wedding and reception, but there would be no way to avoid seeing Dylan and Melissa. I assumed they were still together, at least I hoped they were.

Mac and I were both now in our third year of college, and I was in the process of transferring to Baylor so that we could be together. I was going to finish this fall semester in Houston and then move up during the winter break. We had found a small apartment together that was close to campus and would be perfect for our first place together.

With Rachel's wedding coming up, midterms, and getting ready to move in with Mac, I was beyond busy and stressed out. We had a long weekend coming up for Columbus Day break, and it was also the weekend of Rachel's bridal shower. When going over the guest list with her a few weeks ago, I noticed that Melissa's name wasn't on the list.

"Hey Rachel, isn't Dylan's fiancé invited to your bridal shower? I thought you two were friends, especially because of Dylan." I tried not to sound too interested in her or the fact that she wasn't on the guest list.

"She was invited, but Dylan said she was working and couldn't get the day off. How did you know they got engaged?"

Oops, I should've thought about that. "I actually waited on them right after they got engaged. They were in for dinner with his mom, and he told me they were getting married." Good cover. "Pretty long engagement huh?"

"Well, that's Dylan for ya. To be honest, I'm surprised he actually asked her."

Now, my interest was peaked. "Really? Why do you say that?" I asked.

Rachel knew Dylan better than just about anyone, probably even better than Melissa.

"I don't know, Dylan just never seemed to be the kind of guy that would settle down and get married. He was always such a flirt and a player I guess." She paused, "And a few years ago, he just was acting really strange about Melissa."

I was curious if she knew something and wasn't telling me. "What do you mean?"

"At one point I thought they would break up because he didn't really seem that into her. He took off a couple times and no one really knew where he went, so I kinda thought maybe he was seeing someone else."

"Well, did you ask him?" Now I was getting nervous. "Maybe he just wasn't sure about Melissa."

"He never really was, so I guess that's why I was surprised when they moved in together and even more shocked when they got engaged. Plus, I heard from another friend of ours that she was seeing someone for awhile behind his back. I don't know if Dylan ever found out about it or not."

I was shocked at hearing this. He must not have known or I couldn't imagine he would be okay staying with her if she had been seeing someone behind his back. Although, who was he to talk really?

Rachel cared about Dylan and wanted the best for him. "I hope it's not true. I hate to think that he's marrying someone who was cheating on him. Well, anyway they'll be at the wedding, but she's missing the shower."

Perfect, I thought to myself. At least at the wedding I could avoid them most of the time because there would be so many people there. I was worried about having to be at the shower with Melissa, but thankfully I dodged that bullet.

The weekend of the wedding came and my nerves were starting to get to me. Mac was with me for the weekend, so that definitely helped. He grounded me, and I loved him for that.

He attended the rehearsal dinner with me and we were staying at the hotel the reception would be held for the weekend. When I saw Dylan last year, I didn't tell him that I was dating Mac, but I'm sure he knew from Rachel.

After the rehearsal dinner, Mac and I went to the hotel bar to have a beer and play a game of pool. There were only a handful of stragglers at the bar, so we made ourselves comfortable in the gaming area and he racked up the balls on the pool table.

"Go ahead and break pool shark." He laughed. I was an excellent pool player and he almost never beat me.

As I leaned over the table to take my first shot, he came up behind me and put his arms around me.

I giggled, "You're distracting me!" I turned around and kissed him. "I love you babe."

"I love you too Linds. So tell me, does all this wedding stuff give you any ideas?" He was grinning at me with his gorgeous smile and his eyes were fixed on mine.

"What kind of ideas are you thinking?" I flirted back with him knowing where he was going with his questioning.

"Do you ever see us getting married someday?" He asked.

"Honestly, I never really thought about marriage, before you. I guess I always knew when I was younger that I'd eventually get married and start a family once I was older. But now, it kind of seems like that reality is getting closer all the time."

I couldn't help but think of Dylan in that moment. He was already planning his future with Melissa. I wondered if he ever still thought about me and whether we could've ended up here like Rachel and Troy were if our circumstances were different.

"Hey Linds? Where did you go?"

I realized that I had zoned out for a moment in my thoughts. "Oh, sorry. I was trying to decide on something."

"Really? Anything I can help with?"

"Well," I said, "I was trying to decide whether or not we would elope or have a big wedding." I smiled and kissed him deeply. I truly loved him, and I knew in my heart that I was right where I needed and wanted to be.

The next day I met Rachel and the other bridesmaids for hair and make up in the hotel salon. I returned to the room I was sharing with Mac to get changed into my dress. The dresses were fitted, slimming, and in a beautiful shade of merlot red. When I emerged from the bedroom wearing my dress, Mac's mouth dropped to the floor.

"Wow. Lindsey, you look spectacular!"

I gave him a sexy smile and turned around exposing my bare back where my dress needed zipping. "Can you help me with this?"

"I can help you out of it." He came over to me and slid his hands into my dress and started around to my bare breasts underneath my dress. He kissed the back of my neck and my shoulders and I instantly felt a rush.

"As much as I'd like to continue this, I have to get going." I kissed him and turned around again. "If you help me into it now, I promise I'll let you help me out of it after the reception."

"Deal." He zipped up my dress, kissing me again on the back of my neck. "You're so beautiful Lindsey. Someday you'll be the one in the white dress. And I'll be the luckiest man in the world."

I was so blessed to have this man in my life. After everything I had been through with Michael's death, my parents' divorce, and Dylan, he was the one person in my life that I knew I could always count on to be there for me and never leave. When Michael died, we leaned on each other for support, so when we realized there was an attraction between us, I worried that Michael was the common denominator that held us together. As time passed though, and our relationship grew, I realized that what we had was real. Michael's death may have brought us closer together, but our love was what kept us together.

The ceremony was beautiful, and my sister looked absolutely stunning in her wedding dress. She was so happy that she was glowing, and I could only hope that someday I would be able to walk down the aisle as a bride and be that beautiful.

During the ceremony, I stood at the altar next to the other bridesmaids and I glanced out into the pews of the church at the guests. I tried to not make it so obvious that I was looking for someone in particular, but I was. I caught Mac's eyes and he winked at me making me smile and blush a little. Then, as I was scanning the church, there he was sitting about six rows back, on the aisle, with Melissa by his side. He was looking right at me, and as my eyes met his I felt that same charge rush through me that I always did when I was near him.

He was focused on me and once my eyes locked in on his, he smiled slightly, just enough of that amazingly sexy grin to make me feel it all the way down to my toes. I quickly looked away, knowing that Melissa would no doubt be watching us both closely.

Once the ceremony was over we lined up in the receiving line outside the church to shake hands and hug the guests as they left the church. I was worried about Dylan and Melissa coming through the line, but they must have gone out one of the side doors and bypassed the receiving line altogether. I knew I would have to see them at the reception, but at least I avoided a close encounter.

We spent what seemed like forever posing for pictures for the photographer. Rachel was happier than I had ever seen her, and for the first time in my life I wasn't jealous of her, I was genuinely happy for her. I had always looked up to Rachel, and wanted to be just like her in every way, bringing on feelings of envy and sometimes bitterness that she constantly had more than I did.

But now, as I stood on the arm of the best man I knew, I realized that I had everything I ever wanted. Mac was beyond gorgeous, intelligent, hardworking, and driven. He was romantic, caring, and extremely compassionate. Most of all, he loved me more than anyone ever had before, and I trusted him with my life and my heart.

Regardless of how I felt about Dylan and sometimes still wondered how different things could've been if Michael had never been in that accident, I knew that I was exactly where I was supposed to be. I had always believed in wishing on stars, and though I had never thought I'd have to endure such pain for my wishes to come true, they still did somehow. I had always wished to find happiness and success for myself, and then find someone to share it with.

At the reception, I made sure to take notice of where they were seated and for a moment all I could do was stare at them. As they stood next to their table, his hand was on her lower back and they were leaning in to each other. I watched him whisper something into her ear, and she looked up at him and smiled, then kissed him. Suddenly I felt my heart in my throat, and I could feel my face getting warm.

Just then, Rachel had come up next to me, "Are you okay Linds?"

I broke from my stare, "Yeah, fine. Just feeling a little overwhelmed I guess. I think I need a little air." I turned to leave, but she stopped me.

"Lindsey, what's really going on? You're staring at Dylan and Melissa, and something is clearly bothering you." She reached for my hand, "What aren't you telling me?"

"Today is your day, not mine. I'm sorry. I didn't mean to upset you."

"I'm not upset, I'm just concerned that something is going on with you and I want to help. You're my sister and I love you. I know I haven't always been there for you these past few years the way I should've been and I'm sorry for that."

I felt a tear come down the side of my cheek. "Rachel, you've always been an amazing sister. It's just, there's something I should probably tell you, but I don't know how and I don't think right now is the time or the place." I lowered my head, almost ashamed of the fact that I had kept this from her and here, now, on her wedding day the secret was about to come out.

"Linds, just tell me. How bad can it be?" She wiped the tear from my cheek and put her arm around my shoulder.

"It's about Dylan. And me. A few years ago, we ran into each other at a party back home and he kissed me. It was just one kiss." I could barely look at her. I knew she would be upset with me and I didn't want to disappoint her.

She laughed, "So what? One kiss isn't a big deal. If that's all it was then who cares?" But when I looked up at her, she could already tell by the look on my face that it wasn't just one kiss. "Oh, I'm guessing there's more to it than that?"

"The night I came home from the beach house after Michael, well after we had that fight, Dylan showed up. I guess he was with you when you found out, and he left and came to check on me. He stayed at the house with me, and the next morning, we...well, we were together. Rachel, I always had a crush on him and I thought that's all it would ever be, until I realized that he had feelings for me too. I don't know where it would've gone, because it was over before it started. After Michael's accident I was overcome with grief and guilt for what happened. Michael found Dylan and I together, and a few hours later he was gone. For the longest time I blamed myself."

Rachel just stared at me. "Wow, I had no idea. Why didn't you tell me before now?"

"I didn't want it to complicate anything or change things with you and Dylan. Y'all have been best friends for your entire life and I didn't want it making things awkward."

"I can't believe you and Dylan! I wish you would've told me sooner, so I might have been able to help you two."

"Rachel, there was no way to 'help' us really. It wasn't anything that either of us did or didn't do, it was complete fate. I guess we just weren't meant to be together." I looked at Dylan and Melissa, and then I caught Mac's eye as he was coming toward where we stood talking. "Things worked out just how they were supposed to. It must've been written in the stars, beyond our control. I'm happy. He's happy. Let's just leave it at that."

She hugged me tight, "I love you Linds. I'm so proud of you."

"I love you too. Now go and mingle with your guests and enjoy your amazingly beautiful day!"

Just then Mac joined us. "Wow, look at these two gorgeous women! I think the one in the white dress is taken, so I'll pick you instead." He reached for my hand with that smile on his face that always melted my heart. "Would you like to dance?"

I took his hand, "I thought you'd never ask."

Dylan

She looked even more beautiful than the last time I saw her. I tried not to stare, so as to not upset Melissa. I knew that she would be sensitive to Lindsey being here today and the last thing I wanted to do was make this harder on her. Melissa deserved a lot of credit for coming here today and I had so much respect for her.

We avoided the receiving line, both knowing what the real reason was, but using the excuse that she needed to use the restroom and I didn't want to wait in the long line. Once at the reception, I took notice of where our table was with proximity to the head table, so I would be able to keep Melissa from having to be seated too close to or facing Lindsey the entire night. I realized it was going to be inevitable that we would have to face each other, but I wanted to minimize the interaction.

On our way into the reception I noticed that Lindsey and Mac was at the bar, so I suggested to Melissa that we make our way to congratulate Rachel and Troy. We spent a few moments chatting with them, but didn't want to keep them from a room full of friends and relatives.

As we were standing next to our table, I whispered into Melissa's ear, "I love that dress on you. I'll love it off of you later too."

She smiled and kissed me. I felt like the luckiest man in the room.

After dinner the music started, and when a slow song came on, I asked her to dance. As I held her close and we moved to the music, I couldn't help but notice Lindsey dancing just a few feet away from us. She never mentioned at the restaurant that she had been seeing someone, but once I was able to see his face, I knew exactly who he was. It was Michael's friend that I met at the hospital the night of the accident.

They didn't see us dancing near them, and I watched their body language as they moved. Lindsey lifted her head from his chest and said something to him that made him smile. I saw her face. She was stunning, and she looked happy. She looked like she was in love. Could they actually be together? Or were they here as friends?

I quickly looked away so they wouldn't see me staring at them, and I asked Melissa if she wanted to get another drink from the bar. She needed to use the restroom, so we left the dance floor and went our separate ways for a few minutes.

As I was waiting for our drinks at the bar, he came up next to me and stood.

"Hey, Dylan right?" He asked and extended his hand out to shake mine.

"Yeah, Mac, good to see you again." I reached out and shook his hand, as I wondered if he knew about what happened between Lindsey and I that weekend. "I thought that was you with Lindsey. How've you been?"

"We're good. Busy of course with classes, as I'm sure you can remember from when you were in college. She's transferring up to Baylor for the spring semester, so I've been trying to get things ready in the apartment for her when she moves up during winter break."

So, there it was. They were together, not just friends, and not just dating casually. They were moving in together soon, so obviously their relationship was serious.

"Congratulations. She's an amazing person. You're a lucky guy." I didn't know what else to say to him. Whether he knew about us or not, he was her future and I was her past.

The bartender set his drinks down in front of him, and as he picked them up he turned to me, "Yeah, she's perfect. Don't worry, I'll take good care of her."

He turned and walked away before I could respond. There was nothing for me to say anyway, so I just stood there waiting for Melissa to return from the restroom.

We went back to our table with our drinks and sat down while the speeches were being given and the bride and groom were cutting the cake. I knew I was distracted by Lindsey and Mac, and I tried hard to not let Melissa see it, but she knew me too well.

"Dylan, if you need to talk to her then it's ok. I'm fine with it I promise. Do you have something unresolved with her?"

"No, it's not like that at all. I guess, I just wish we could go back and erase what happened."

"Why? You obviously had feelings for her, so why would you say that?"

I wasn't quite sure how to answer that question. "Well, I suppose part of it is that I could take away the hurt I caused you if I could go back. And I'd be able to just go back to treating Lindsey like Rachel's little sister and we could still be friends."

"You'll never be able to be friends again unfortunately because you two crossed that line. But if you need some closure with her, then get it. Do what you need to do so we can keep moving forward."

I leaned in and kissed her on the cheek, "You are truly the most amazing woman." Melissa was confident and mature and finally secure enough in our relationship to be able to trust me again.

She was also right, I needed closure with Lindsey. We didn't end because we wanted to end. In fact, we never even got a chance to get started because fate got in the way. I wanted Lindsey to know that I didn't not choose her. I never made a choice at all, except to give her the space I thought she needed.

She touched my hand on the table, "I'm going to go up to our room and freshen up a little. I'll get us a drink from the bar on my way back, and you can sweep me off my feet and onto the dance floor when I return."

I knew what she was doing. "Are you sure?"

She smiled and rose from the table, leaned down and kissed me passionately on the lips, "I'm sure. Just don't forget who you're going home with tonight." She gave me a sexy grin and turned to leave.

I walked to the dance floor with my heart beating faster with each step I took toward them. Lindsey and Mac were slow dancing, and as I approached them, she looked at me and immediately froze in place. Mac looked up to see me standing next to them.

"Sorry to interrupt, but would it be okay if I cut in for this dance?" I was addressing him, but my eyes were fixed on her.

Mac looked down at Lindsey, and she instantly snapped her eyes to his. Without looking at me he answered, "That's completely her call."

She looked at me and back up at him. "Mac, I think maybe Dylan and I need a few minutes to talk." He kissed her on the cheek, glanced at me, and walked away.

I held my hand out to her and she placed hers in mine. She stepped into my arms and I pulled her close to me. For a few minutes we danced without saying anything, holding each other close. I could feel her heart beating against my chest, and I wondered if she could feel mine racing as I tried to find the words I needed to say to her.

I stopped moving and she lifted her head from my chest. There were things I needed to say to her before I let her go, forever.

Lindsey

As I saw Dylan walking toward us, I felt my heart start beating faster. I wasn't sure how Mac would react, and the last thing I wanted was any kind of scene at my sister's wedding. I saw them talking to each other at the bar earlier, but Mac didn't say anything to me so I didn't bring it up to him.

I lifted my head from Mac's chest.

Dylan's piercing eyes were fixed on me as he spoke. "Sorry to interrupt, but would it be okay if I cut in for this dance?"

Mac spoke to Dylan, but was looking down at me. "That's completely her call."

"Mac, I think maybe Dylan and I need a few minutes to talk."

He kissed me on the cheek and then walked away leaving me alone with Dylan on the dance floor. His hand stretched out to me and I placed mine in his and stepped into his arms.

I placed my head on his chest and breathed him in as we swayed slowly, closely to the music. His heart was beating, probably as fast as mine.

After a few minutes, I lifted my head to look into his eyes. "Was there a reason for cutting in?"

"So, you and Mac, huh? Didn't see that one coming."

"Dylan, I really don't think that's any of your business," I said defensively. I had worried for too long about what other people thought of Mac and me ending up together after Michael's death, and I wasn't going to be made to feel bad by him of all people.

"I'm sorry, I wasn't trying to upset you. I guess I'm just surprised. When did the two of you start dating?"

"He took me to senior prom and we've been together ever since that night." I wanted to tell Dylan all of the emotions I was feeling being here in his arms again, but what good would that do? We were both with other people, I was moving in with Mac, and he and Melissa were getting married. "I'm happy Dylan. He loves me, and I love him."

He touched my chin and lifted my head so my eyes could meet his. "That's all I could ever want for you Linds. I just wish I could've been the one to make you happy."

My heart was starting to beat faster, his skin still touching my face and his other hand firmly placed on the small of my back, our bodies still touching.

"Maybe you could've, but fate stepped in and changed our path." I felt my eyes starting to well up, and the last thing I wanted was for him to see me cry. "I made so many wishes so many nights and I guess they just didn't come true."

"I think you're wrong Lindsey. They did come true. The stars were already written long before you made those wishes, long before you and I came together. I truly believe that we crossed paths for a reason, but maybe it wasn't the reason that we thought or that you wished for."

A tear fell and he wiped it away.

"Then why Dylan? Tell me why we were brought together only to be ripped apart because of circumstances that we couldn't control. The accident changed everything."

"It did. It changed our paths and put us both in the direction we were supposed to be in, leading us to where we needed to be all along."

He leaned down and kissed my cheek, and then the freckle on my nose.

I smiled, "You and that freckle."

"Sorry, can't help it." He smiled and pulled me close again into his arms. We danced for a few more minutes until long after the song was over.

I lifted my head again, "Dylan, it would've been you. I wanted it to be you all along. But I just wasn't ready and I didn't want to hold you back. I'm sorry, I should've told you a long time ago."

"I wanted it to be me. But since it couldn't be me, then I'm thankful you have him. All I want is for you to be happy and loved."

"I am." I smiled at him and hugged him tight.

We both caught a glimpse of Rachel as she was watching us on the dance floor together right now.

"Oh boy, I think we're going to be in trouble with someone." He gestured to where Rachel was standing with her eyes on us.

"She knows. I told her."

We both laughed a little and Dylan, in typical Dylan fashion leaned in to whisper in my ear, "Should we really set her over the edge?" He leaned back and gave me that grin of his, the one that gets me every time.

"I think maybe we shouldn't." I smiled back at him. "The last thing we need is for the bride to be angry on her wedding day. Besides, I think there are two other people in this room right now that I'm more worried about upsetting."

Dylan put his hands on the side of my face, leaned in and kissed me gently on the lips. He lingered just long enough for the energy to generate all the way through me.

"Be happy, short stack."

He turned and left me standing there, just like he had all those years before. This time though, I knew where I was going from this moment and I knew I would be okay.